THE MAGIC SHOP BOOKS
by Bruce Coville

The Monster's Ring
Russell Crannaker, bullied all his life,
gets a chance to fight back when he is given
a monstrous magical item.

Jeremy Thatcher, Dragon Hatcher
Jeremy Thatcher's deepest desires take flight
when he is forced to raise a demanding
dragon hatchling.

Jennifer Murdley's Toad
Jennifer Murdley, a girl "in a plain brown wrapper,"
buys a talking toad who knows a thing or two about
the true nature of beauty.

The Skull of Truth
Charlie Eggleston, who can't help lying,
suddenly must tell the truth and nothing *but* when
he takes the Skull from Mr. Elives' shop.

The Skull of Truth

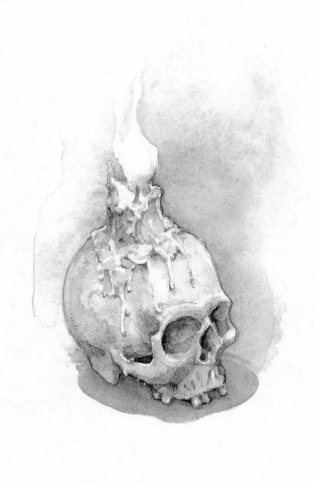

The Skull of Truth

+❖+

A MAGIC SHOP BOOK

Bruce Coville

ILLUSTRATED BY
GARY A. LIPPINCOTT

HARCOURT, INC.

SAN DIEGO   NEW YORK   LONDON

www.HarcourtBooks.com

Illustrations copyright © 1997 by Gary A. Lippincott

Library of Congress Cataloging-in-Publication Data
Coville, Bruce.
The skull of truth/Bruce Coville; illustrated by Gary A. Lippincott.
p. cm.
"A Magic Shop Book."
Summary: Charlie, a sixth-grader with a compulsion to tell lies,
acquires a mysterious skull that forces its owner to tell only the truth,
causing some awkward moments before he understands its power.
[1. Honesty—Fiction. 2. Family life—Fiction. 3. Schools—Fiction.
4. Friendship—Fiction.] I. Lippincott, Gary A., ill. II. Title.
PZ7.C8344Sk 2002
[Fic]—dc21 2002024244
ISBN 0-15-204612-7

Text set in New Baskerville
Designed by Lydia D'moch

C E G H F D B

Printed in the United States of America

For Frank Hodge,
friend of books, friend of young readers

Contents

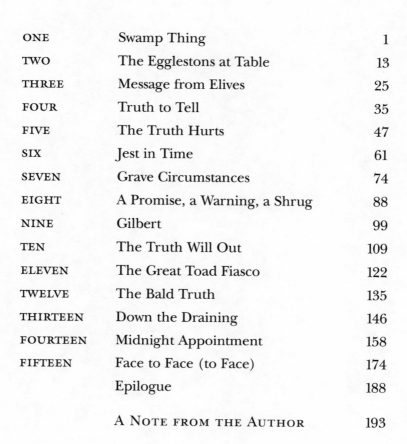

ONE

Swamp Thing

Charlie Eggleston looked at the frog he held cupped in his hands. "Want to go home now?" he asked gently.

The frog did not answer, which was not really a surprise.

Charlie knelt and opened his hands anyway. The frog took three long leaps into Tucker's Swamp, disappearing with a final *plunk!* under a mat of algae.

Wiping his hands on his jeans, Charlie took a deep breath. He loved the smell of this place—loved everything about it, for that matter: the great willows with their drooping branches and trunks so big his arms could barely reach halfway around them; the familiar paths—sometimes a narrow strip of solid ground, sometimes no more than a string of squishy hummocks; the shallow pools filled with frogs and salamanders. Most of all he loved the sense of magic that hovered over the swamp, the feeling that something deep and strange here had resisted being civilized.

A familiar lump of anger lodged itself halfway between his stomach and his throat. He couldn't believe Mark Evans's father was going to drain the swamp and turn it into an "industrial park." He snorted at the words. People always accused him of lying, but the very phrase *industrial park* was a whopper that beat any he had ever told. How could a collection of factories be called a *park*?

Glancing around, Charlie wondered if it was safe to leave the swamp yet. His mother would be angry if he didn't get home soon. But if he left before Mark and his gang had given up waiting for him, he might never get home at all.

The buzz of insects filled the air. A mosquito began drilling a hole in his neck. He slapped at it. When he brought his hand away the insect's flimsy body lay crushed in his palm, its head and thread-thin legs extending from the small blot of Charlie's own blood that marked where its abdomen had been.

"Little vampire," muttered Charlie, reminding himself that he didn't actually love *everything* about the swamp.

He turned to go, stirring up a small cloud of yellow butterflies as he pushed his way through a patch of ferns. A water snake slithered off the path and into a murky pool. Life seemed to pulse all around him, and the idea that someone was going to destroy the swamp made him sick all over again.

That was why he had made up the story that got him in so much trouble with Mark today: to protect the swamp. *Besides,* he told himself, *just because I don't have the facts to prove it doesn't mean what I said wasn't true. I bet it really is.*

Charlie was dragging his bike from the brush pile where he had hidden it when a familiar voice sneered, "Well, look here—it's Charlie Eggleston, king of the liars."

Charlie felt his stomach clench. If he didn't get away fast, Mark and his cronies were apt to turn him into something resembling roadkill.

Swinging onto his bike, he began to pedal.

One of Mark's friends appeared ahead of him.

Charlie swerved to the right to avoid him but found his path blocked by another of Mark's pals.

"Get him!" cried Mark—rather unnecessarily, thought Charlie, since the gang was already working pretty hard at doing just that.

Charlie spun his bike and headed straight for the swamp. Shouting and screaming, the others charged after him. Under normal circumstances they would probably have caught him. But with fear as his fuel, Charlie was able to outdistance them, if only by a few feet. At the edge of the swamp he cast aside his bike and plunged in, splashing through the murky water, not caring where the paths were, what he stepped in, whether he was going to ruin his sneakers. The terror was on him, and he had to get away.

He could hear Mark and the others splashing in behind him but dared not glance back to see how close they were. Heart pounding, he raced through water that reached past his knees. He knew his mother would be furious when she saw his swamp-soaked pants, and even as he fled Mark's vengeance some small part of his mind was inventing an alibi to offer when he got home.

The voices began to fade behind him. Mark's shouted "I'll teach you to lie about my father, you snot-faced baby!" were the last words Charlie actually made out.

He was gasping now, and the breath burned in his lungs. Looking around, he found he had entered a part of the swamp he had never seen before. He felt a little tingle of fear, until he realized that since he had abandoned all the regular paths he *should* be someplace new. Tucker's Swamp wasn't that big, so if he kept going he would have to find his way out sooner or later—though if it was later he would probably be in even more trouble at home for not showing up in time for supper. His father was big on having the whole family sit down together.

He slogged on, hoping his favorite daydreams—the ones about weird creatures that lived in the swamp—were really only fantasies after all, and that he wouldn't find anything too large or too strange before he made his way out again.

The swamp turned out to be bigger than Charlie had realized. Even so, he didn't start to panic until he noticed the sun getting low in the sky. The orange and pink that smeared the horizon were spectacular, but their awesome beauty announced a fast-approaching darkness, and he had no desire to be wading through the swamp once that darkness arrived.

A flutter of wings made Charlie look up. Was it dark enough for bats to be out yet? He shivered, and moved on.

Somewhere to his right he heard the hoot of an owl. When he turned to see if he could spot the bird, he noticed a strip of dry land.

Maybe that *will get me out of here!* he thought eagerly.

Filled with new hope, he squished toward it.

The swarming mosquitoes were thicker now, and he was constantly slapping at his neck and arms. The evening chill had settled, and his wet legs were freezing. What a relief it was to see a glow of lights ahead! He began to hurry along the path.

Another hundred yards brought him to the edge of the swamp. He crossed a grassy area, came to a road, and looked around expectantly. The chill that rippled through him this time had nothing to do with the dropping temperature. *Where am I?* He had been all the way around Tucker's Swamp dozens of times and had no recollection of ever seeing this spot.

Much as he dreaded what his parents would say, Charlie decided he had better call home to see if they would come and get him. That decision made, he set off along the road to his left, where the lights seemed closest, hoping to find a pay phone.

Mist curled around his feet. Wisps of it rose before him like beckoning fingers.

Charlie shuddered. Wishing he had not abandoned his bike, he began to walk faster.

A moment later he found himself standing in front of a store he had never seen before. That wouldn't have bothered him if the store had looked brand-new. But this store looked old—very old indeed—and that was a little frightening.

Even so, the place was so fascinating that he couldn't resist stepping up to look through its window. That window, divided into many small sections by thin strips of wood, curved out from the front of the store. Printed on the glass in old-fashioned lettering were the words:

ELIVES' MAGIC SUPPLIES
S. H. ELIVES, PROP.

A small bell tinkled overhead as he stepped inside.

Charlie began to smile. The shop was filled—crammed, really—with great stuff. Chains of jewel-colored silk scarves draped gracefully from the ceiling. Every available surface—not just the tabletops and the countertops but the walls and most of the floor as well—was cluttered with magicians' paraphernalia. To his right he saw a whole wallful of cages. Some held doves and rabbits—for pulling out of hats, he assumed. But the majority of the cages

held a weird assortment of lizards, toads, snakes, bats, and spiders.

Charlie wondered if this Elives guy collected them from the swamp, or if they were some kind of special animals.

Straight ahead was a large wooden box for sawing people in half. Charlie chuckled. It would be fun to try that on Mark. Especially if it didn't work.

To his left was a glass display case that held— among other things—big decks of cards, Chinese rings, and little books that hinted at ancient secrets. At the far end of the case was a human skull labeled THE SKULL OF TRUTH.

Cool, thought Charlie.

At the back of the shop stretched a long counter made of dark wood. A wonderfully detailed dragon was carved into the front.

On top of the counter sat an old-fashioned brass cash register.

On top of the cash register sat a stuffed owl.

At least, Charlie thought it was stuffed—until it turned toward him, blinked, then uttered a series of low hoots.

Behind the counter was a doorway covered by a beaded curtain. From beyond that curtain came a voice that reminded Charlie of the wind whispering through the willow trees in the swamp. "Peace, Uwila. He can wait until I finish this spell."

"It's all right!" shouted Charlie. "I'm in no hurry. I just—"

His words were cut off by a small explosion at the

back of the shop. A cloud of sour-smelling green smoke drifted through the beaded curtain, accompanied by some muttered cursing.

"Do you need help?" called Charlie.

"Don't be silly! I'll be out in a moment."

Charlie shrugged. He only had a dollar or two in his pocket—almost certainly not enough to buy anything here—so as far as he was concerned the longer the man took the better, since the odds were good that once he realized Charlie was just looking and not buying he would throw him out.

A wet sound caught Charlie's attention. He looked down and groaned. His chances of getting thrown out would be even higher if the shopkeeper noticed he was dripping swamp water all over the floor.

Eager to distance himself from the small puddle that had formed beneath him, Charlie crossed to the glass display case.

He found himself staring at the skull. Its lower jaw was missing, which somehow made it seem even spookier than it normally would have. It gave Charlie a delicious thrill to think this bony thing had once been *inside* the head of a living person.

"Like that, do you?" asked a voice close to his ear.

Charlie jumped again. Turning, he found himself face-to-face with a man no taller than himself, and so old that the wrinkles in his walnut-colored skin probably qualified as historic landmarks. He had dark, astonishing eyes and white hair that hung loosely about his shoulders. Charlie noticed a smudge of green above one bushy white eyebrow.

"I said: 'Like that?' "

Charlie nodded.

The old man—Mr. Elives, he supposed—gave him a sly grin. "Well, it's not for sale. Now, what are you here for?"

He asked the question in such an intense voice that Charlie hesitated before he said, "Do you have a phone I could use?"

The old man shook his head. "I don't have any use for such things."

"Not even a pay phone?"

The old man narrowed his eyes. "You heard me the first time. Now, why have you come here? No one enters this shop by accident. No one comes here to use a pay phone. No one comes here just to 'look around.' What do you *need*, boy?"

Charlie thought for a second. "Do you have a spell for getting rid of bullies?"

"Not one that you can afford," replied the old man, as if he really did have one.

Charlie smiled. He appreciated that kind of answer—though he would have appreciated the spell even more. "Then I guess I don't need anything. Though I might buy that skull if I could afford it. Can I take a closer look?"

"Bend down and put your face to the glass. You'll see everything you need to see."

Startled by the old man's rudeness, Charlie was trying to decide whether to make some smart comment in response when another explosion rattled the back of the shop.

"Fraxit," muttered the old man. Moving faster than Charlie would have thought possible, he turned and hurried back through the beaded curtain.

Charlie stood for a moment, wondering if he should follow the old man to see if he needed help. Finally he decided to stay put and do just as the shopkeeper had suggested instead. Kneeling, he pressed his face to the glass to take a closer look at the skull.

A chill skittered down his spine. The dark eye sockets, so big they looked as though you could tuck a duck's egg into each of them, seemed to stare directly into his. Charlie felt something stir inside him, and recognized it as a deep desire to possess the skull. Maybe he could use it the next time his mother got on him about the way he made up stories. When she moaned "*Why* can't you tell the truth, Charlie?" (as she did nearly every day) he would hold up the skull and say, "This is the Skull of Truth. Do you want me to end up like him?"

He smiled. That was a good idea.

Pressing his face close to the glass again, he whispered, "Want to come home with me?"

He jumped back with a shout as he felt a kind of buzzing in his brain.

Charlie shook his head to clear it, then stared at the skull nervously. A second later he did something that astonished him. For though he lied constantly, Charlie Eggleston had never stolen anything in his life, had never even had the desire to do so. So it was almost as if someone else's legs were carrying him behind the counter, someone else's hands sliding open the unlocked wooden door, someone else's fingers reaching into the glass case to lift the skull from the polished wooden base on which it was mounted.

What am I doing? thought Charlie in horror, as he drew the grisly item from the case.

His horror increased tenfold when he heard the rustle of beads that signaled the old man coming back. How could he possibly explain? He would be arrested for shoplifting!

His heart pounding with panic, Charlie looked around wildly. He spotted a door at the side of the shop. Spurred by fear, he bolted for it, tore it open, and shot through into the darkness.

TWO

The Egglestons
at Table

To his astonishment, Charlie found himself standing next to his bicycle, back where he had entered the swamp. That was bizarre and upsetting— but not as bad as the realization that he was still holding the skull. He thought he had dropped it before he raced out the door. He certainly hadn't intended to steal the thing. He didn't even really want it!

He thought about setting it on the ground and walking away. But somehow that seemed disrespectful of whoever it had once belonged to. And just throwing it into the swamp would be even worse.

His heart pounding, Charlie cradled the horrid object in his hands. The dome was textured like an eggshell, only thicker and more solid. The teeth of the upper jaw felt sharp and jagged where they rested against his palm. Turning it over, he saw a quarter-size hole, and realized that was where the skull had once been connected to its spine.

He wondered what face the skull had once worn. Had it been male, or female? With the flesh stripped away and only bare bones left, holding it was like holding a reminder that death waits for everyone.

Charlie shuddered. What was he going to do with the thing? If he took it home, he would have to invent some story to explain to his mother where he had gotten it. She certainly wouldn't believe the truth—not that she ever heard it from Charlie anyway. But in this case even *he* wouldn't believe the truth. That old man and his shop were just too weird.

Well, weird or not, he was going to have to figure out some way to take the skull back. Normally, going back to a store wouldn't be that hard, though in this case it might be a bit embarrassing. The thing was, he didn't know if he could even find the place again. It wasn't like he could look it up in the yellow pages; the old man had made it clear he didn't have a telephone.

Charlie sighed. Whatever he finally decided to do with the skull, he had better get home now. He was going to be in enough trouble as it was, especially when his mother saw his wet pants, swamp-stained halfway up his thighs. He wasn't supposed to get wet at all when he came down here, much less go wading. The fact that he had been running for his life wouldn't make much difference to her. Maybe he could think of a story to cover that on the way home, too.

He looked for a way to attach the skull to his bike but couldn't find any. Finally, reluctantly, he tucked it inside his jacket. It was only then, when he felt its smooth weight against his stomach, that the full horror of the thing hit him.

He was carrying a human skull!

Jumping on his bike, he pedaled for all he was worth, away from the swamp, away from the magic shop; away from the entire horrible afternoon.

The Eggleston family lived in a rambling old ivy-covered house on the edge of town. They had moved here when Charlie was in kindergarten, and Mrs. Eggleston had been working on restoring the place ever since. She was constantly stripping the paint off old woodwork and trying to bring it back to what she called "its original beauty."

Despite her efforts, the house had the kind of look that tended to inspire rumors about ghosts and hauntings. The fact that its backyard bordered on the town cemetery did nothing to discourage those rumors.

Neither did Charlie. Over the years he had reported numerous ghostly happenings to his class-mates—all of them, of course, completely the products of his imagination. The truth was, he had gotten so used to the cemetery that it held little terror for him now. In fact, he liked to go there when-ever he wanted to be alone.

It was almost seven-thirty when Charlie reached his home. Stewbone, the family's ancient springer spaniel, barked a friendly greeting from the front porch.

"Shhh!" said Charlie. "I don't want them to know I'm here."

Stewbone lay back down, put his head on his paws, and gazed at Charlie mournfully.

Charlie walked his bike quietly up the driveway, past his mother's blue pickup truck and his father's maroon van. Painted on the side of the van were the words EGGLESTON'S MEAT MARKET along with a big picture of a dancing cow, which Charlie had always thought was kind of sick. The truck and the van were in the driveway because Charlie's mother had long ago taken over the garage—a ramshackle old structure originally built as a horse barn—for her furniture refinishing business. Though the walls were sagging and the roof had a coat of moss that Mrs. Eggleston was constantly nagging her husband to do something about, Charlie liked the building just the way it was.

He slipped inside. Walking past benches covered with brushes, scrapers, and chemical strippers, he made his way to a rickety ladder at the back of the garage. The ladder led to a low attic, which was where Charlie had decided he would stash the skull. He figured getting rid of it before he went into the house would save him at least one set of explanations.

When Charlie left the garage he spotted his mother waiting at the back door of the house. She was tapping a wooden spoon against her forehead and muttering, "Charlie, Charlie, Charlie."

This, he knew, was not a good sign.

Stewbone was sitting beside her, wagging his tail.

"Traitor," muttered Charlie.

Stewbone trotted over and licked his hand.

When Charlie got to the door his mother stopped tapping the spoon against her own forehead and used it to give him a sharp tap on his. "Did you forget that Gramma Ethel and Uncle Bennie were coming over for dinner this evening?"

"I didn't forget!" he said indignantly, though in truth it had completely slipped his mind.

"Then where have you been? Never mind! Tell me later. Right now get upstairs and get cleaned up. Good grief, look at your pants. Don't let your father see those or you'll be grounded for a week. On the other hand, maybe I'll tell him about them myself. I'm a little tired of covering up for you, Charlie."

"It wasn't my—"

"None of your excuses! Just get changed. If you hurry, you can join us for dessert, which will make your grandmother feel better. It may also get her off my case—something you *are* going to pay for, bub."

She gave him a swat on the rear with the spoon as he hurried past. "And be quick about it!"

Then she scurried through the kitchen, back into the dining room. Charlie could hear his father's deep laugh and the delighted squeals of his little sisters, Tiffany and Mimi.

He sighed and trudged up the back stairs.

In his room Charlie stripped out of his wet pants and sneakers, then went next door to the bathroom to wash his hands. When he thought about what he had been handling, what he had just stored in the garage, he washed them twice more to be safe.

Five minutes later he clattered down the front stairs and entered the dining room as if nothing had happened.

"Hey, Charlie!" said Uncle Bennie, who was about to tuck a piece of lemon pie into his mouth. "I missed your sparkling conversation."

"I had an important Scout meeting," lied Charlie, quickly and easily. "I couldn't miss it, because we're planning a first-aid demonstration for the county fair, and I'm in charge."

Actually he had quit Scouts six months ago, though he couldn't remember now whether he had told his mother or not.

"That's nice," said Uncle Bennie. He sounded totally unconvinced, which made Charlie feel indignant.

"Don't those Scout boys care about your family?" asked Gramma Ethel.

Gramma Ethel was really Charlie's great-grandmother. She had been married to Grampa Albert, who had delighted and amazed Charlie by playing Pull-My-Finger every time he came to dinner, until it was time for Charlie to enter kindergarten, and Mrs. Eggleston had made him stop. Three years ago Grampa Albert had died unexpectedly of a digestive problem one night after a holiday dinner. Since then, Uncle Bennie had been in charge of bringing Gramma Ethel to family gatherings.

"Andy Simmons ate a bug today," put in Charlie's youngest sister, Mimi, who was in kindergarten now herself. "Then he spit it out. It was gross."

She looked very pleased with herself. Charlie wondered if the story had any truth to it. He still hadn't figured out how to tell when Mimi was fibbing.

"He did not," said Tiffany, who was in third grade. "You're just making that up."

"Am not," said Mimi. "I saved a piece. You want to see it?" She put down her fork and began digging in her pocket.

"That's enough, girls!" said Mr. Eggleston sharply. "Charlie, sit down and eat your supper. Your mother dished up a plate for you. It's cold, but that's what happens when you don't get home on time."

Charlie sighed. It would be perfectly easy for him to pop his plate into the microwave and warm it up. But Mr. Eggleston had had to eat cold meals if he was late when he was a kid, and he figured Charlie should be held to the same standard.

Charlie took his place next to his uncle and stared at the cold beef stew. It reminded him of the swamp.

"Sorry you weren't here earlier, old man," said Bennie, putting a friendly hand on his shoulder. "I've got to leave in a few minutes. I'm starting a new class tonight."

Charlie sighed again. Uncle Bennie was his favorite relative. He always had some new trick to demonstrate, or a new joke that Charlie could take to school the next day. Bennie got a lot of them from his roommate, Dave, who worked at the TV station over in Edgemont.

"What is it this time, Bennie?" asked Mr. Eggleston cheerfully. "Underwater basket weaving? How to make a fur coat from your cat's hairballs?"

"Archie!" snapped Mrs. Eggleston.

Bennie made a face at his brother-in-law. "The class is in storytelling. This fabulous storyteller just moved to town—she's the new children's librarian, Charlie—and she's teaching a class at the Evans Memorial Building."

"I'd like to learn to tell stories," said Charlie.

"You don't do anything *but* tell stories," said Gramma Ethel. "Good grief, boy, you wouldn't know the truth if it snuck up and bit you on your heinie."

"Gramma!" said Mrs. Eggleston sharply.

"Well, it's a fact," said Gramma Ethel. "Mark my words, Veronica: If that boy doesn't learn to tell the truth soon, he'll come to no good end."

Charlie pushed back his chair and ran from the table.

"There," said his mother. "Now see what you've done!"

"Oh, fiddlesticks," said Gramma Ethel. "If the boy can't take the truth he should get out of the frying pan."

———

Charlie flopped onto his bed and stared at the wall, trying to think of things he should have said to his grandmother. The problem was, she was right—which made it really hard to come up with a snappy comeback. He had had a terrible problem telling the truth ever since The Great Toad Fiasco (as his mother liked to call it) back in second grade. He just couldn't seem to stop himself from lying. He would open his mouth, and out would pop a whopper.

Restless, he got up and began to wander around the room, which he kept unusually tidy for a boy of his age. He was poking at his pebble collection when his mother knocked at the door and peered around the frame. "May I enter?"

Charlie shrugged. "If you really want to."

Mrs. Eggleston rolled her eyes. "No, I hate visiting my firstborn child." She came in and sat on the edge of his bed. "I don't know where you got your neatness gene from," she said, glancing around the room, "but I wish we could figure out some way to inoculate your father with it."

Charlie smiled.

"So what happened this afternoon?" asked his mother.

A strange panic seized him. He actually *wanted* to tell his mother about his weird experience in the swamp. But if he told her the truth, he knew she would think he was lying. Heck, if he hadn't been there himself, *he* would think he was lying. He was silent for a moment, trying to decide what to say.

"Charlie?"

He shrugged again. "Mark Evans and some of the guys tried to beat me up."

Mrs. Eggleston looked troubled. "Any specific reason?"

Now, this was an answer Charlie *didn't* want to give her. The story he had concocted in class that morning, about what was going to happen if Mark's father drained Tucker's Swamp, had seemed to make sense at the moment. Now that he was no longer in the grip of his passionate anger, Charlie could see he had gone over the top when he claimed it would make all the town's wells run dry and cause the immediate extinction of three endangered species.

"It was a mob hit."

"Charlie, if you don't give me a straight answer I can't help you." His mother's voice was soft, concerned.

"You can't help me anyway," snapped Charlie. "Not unless you can stop Mark Evans's father from draining the swamp."

A light of understanding went on in Mrs. Eggleston's face. "I think it's a terrible idea, too, honey," she said gently. "I just don't know that there's anything we can do about it. And the town does need the jobs, now that the paper mill is closed."

She started to say something else, but just then Mimi and Tiffany got into a screaming fight, and she had to go mediate, leaving Charlie alone in his room.

Suddenly he realized that he was exhausted. The trouble at school, the race through the swamp, the weird scene in the old man's store, and the fuss at home had all taken their toll.

Even so, sleep did not come easily. Charlie's rebellious mind insisted on replaying the day's events over and over. It was well past eleven when he finally drifted into a restless sleep—and less than an hour after that when he was roused by someone knocking on his window.

Charlie opened his eyes and gasped.

Two rats were peering in at him. The smaller of the pair had its face pressed to the window. Its companion was standing on its hind legs, tapping the glass with its paws. It whacked the glass several times, clearly getting more and more frustrated. Finally, in a small but fiercely insistent voice, it shouted, "Charlie Eggleston, you silly twit! Open the window and let us in!"

THREE

Message from Elives

Charlie's first response was to pull the covers over his head, hoping that if he ignored the rats, they would go away—or that he might move on to a different dream.

It didn't work. The larger rat continued to pound on the glass. The sound was faint, not much louder than rain pattering against the window. But it was impossible to ignore.

Charlie considered leaping out of bed and running to get his parents. However, he was fairly certain they wouldn't believe him if he told them he had been frightened by a pair of rats trying to convince him to open his window. Even if he did manage to get his parents to come into his room—by pretending he was sick, or something—he figured the rats would make it a point not to let themselves be seen.

The tiny pounding stopped.

Moving slowly, scarcely breathing, Charlie lowered the edge of the sheet just enough to see the window.

The smaller rat had risen onto its hind legs and was whispering in the other rat's ear. The big rat made a face but shrugged and dropped to its haunches.

"Charlie!" called the second rat, speaking in a much more pleasant voice than the big rat had used. "Charlie, please let us in. We need to talk to you."

"About what?" he asked, without lowering the sheet any farther.

"We have a message for you."

"From who?"

"Mr. Elives."

"I didn't mean to steal the skull!" cried Charlie desperately. "He can have it back!"

Realizing he was pleading with a rat, he began to blush.

"He doesn't want the skull back," said the larger rat impatiently. "At least, not yet. He just wants you to have some information about it."

Charlie sighed. Maybe he *should* get up and talk to the rats. After all, if they could be heard through the glass, they could certainly give him the message without coming through the window. Cautiously he pulled aside the covers and climbed out of bed. As he crept toward the window he realized he was actually more frightened now than he had been that afternoon in the magic shop.

He knelt in front of the sill. Speaking softly but clearly, he said, "What's the message?"

"Let us in," said the bigger rat.

"That's not the message!"

"No, but we have to come in to give it to you."

"Why?"

"Because it's a *written* message," said the smaller rat.

The big rat turned and reached over the sill. When it turned back, it was clutching a rolled-up piece of yellowed paper.

Charlie wondered briefly where the paper had come from, then decided it must have been tucked into the ivy that twined up the side of the house. "Read it to me," he said.

The big rat shook its head.

"Then hold it up to the window, and I'll read it myself."

"No can do, Charlie. We have to get you to sign a receipt to prove the message was actually delivered. If you don't open the window and let us in, we'll just take it back to Elives. Then see what kind of a fix you've gotten yourself into!"

Charlie bit his finger. The pain told him he was definitely awake. So this was no dream. Yet weird as the situation was, curiosity was starting to overcome fear. Even more compelling, he had a feeling the message truly was important. But he'd had pet rodents before, and he knew how quickly they could slip through small spaces. If he opened the window enough for the rats to pass in the message, they might let themselves in, too.

Of course, he could always slam the window on

them. Except killing a talking rat felt like murder, somehow.

He stared at them. "You don't have rabies or anything, do you?"

The smaller rat made a squeak of outrage. "Charlie Eggleston! Don't be vulgar! Now, open this window and let us in."

Feeling as if he had no choice, Charlie pushed the window up a few inches.

The two rats slipped through the opening.

"That's better," said the smaller one, in a friendly voice. "My name is Roxanne." She pointed at the larger rat. "And this is Jerome."

Jerome nodded but said nothing; he was clearly still miffed by Charlie's reluctance to let them in.

"How come you can talk?" asked Charlie.

"It's a long story," replied Jerome, "and really none of your business. *Your* business is this."

While Jerome handed Charlie the rolled-up paper he had pulled from the ivy, his female companion slipped back through the open window. She returned with another piece of paper. With Jerome holding down one end, she unrolled it. "Sign here," she said.

"What is it?" asked Charlie.

"Confirmation of delivery," said Jerome. "I told you, we need it to show the boss."

"Do I have to sign it in blood or anything?"

Jerome sighed. "Ballpoint pen will be fine."

"Just a minute. I'll get one from my desk."

As Charlie turned to get the pen he heard Jerome mutter, "What a doofus!"

"Shhhh!" hissed Roxanne.

Charlie blushed but said nothing. Returning with the pen, he bent to read the receipt. Printed in shaky handwriting were the words "I, Charlie Eggleston, do hereby confirm and acknowledge that I have received from Roxanne and Jerome the message regarding The Skull of Truth." At the bottom was a line for his signature. Wishing he had a lawyer, he read the note three times. It didn't seem to promise anything or incriminate him for taking the skull. He decided to go ahead and sign it. For one thing, it was probably the only way to get rid of the rats.

After he had written his signature, he said to Roxanne (he was not at all comfortable with Jerome), "Who is that old man, anyway?"

The rat laughed, a surprisingly pretty sound. "Some questions are better left unanswered, Charlie." Then she slipped back through the window.

Jerome followed close behind.

Turning, they stood and waved to him. "Good luck!" called Roxanne. *"Be careful!"*

Then they disappeared over the sill.

As he watched them go, Charlie noticed a short, dumpy-looking girl standing on the sidewalk in front of the house. When he saw the rats scamper across the lawn a moment later, he expected the girl to scream and run away. To his surprise, she knelt and picked them up, gently placing one on each shoulder.

The rats appeared to be whispering in her ears. The girl laughed, a clear, happy sound that made

Charlie feel good despite how frightened he was. But when she stood up and began to walk away, a cloud of mist enveloped her.

After about ten steps she simply disappeared.

Charlie shivered and remained staring out the window for a long time. Finally he turned and picked up the paper the rats had left with him. He noticed that his fingers were trembling as he unrolled it.

Printed across the top of the page in big, bold letters were the words IMPORTANT INFORMATION. At the bottom was a drawing of a skull. Between them, written in the same shaky cursive as the receipt, was the following:

To: Charlie Eggleston
From: S. H. Elives
Regarding: The Skull of Truth

Mr. Eggleston,

It appears you did a most unwise thing this afternoon. While you may fear I will be angry with you—and I certainly have good reason to be, considering that you took an item from my shop without paying for it—the truth is, my immediate reaction is relief that the skull is no longer my problem.

My second reaction is to feel some concern. Though some former customers might tell you that this is an unusual response, this is an unusual situation. You have taken into your hands what I consider to be the most dangerous item in my

31

shop. What will happen when it is unleashed on the world I cannot say.

I can, however, offer you some advice and a few words of warning.

First: Be careful what you say.

Second: Be careful to whom you say it.

Third: Remember that often it is smarter to say nothing at all.

Finally: Under no circumstances should you let the skull out of your possession!

It will be a while before I can come back to your area. When I do, I will expect you to return the skull to me in good condition. Failure to do so will be to risk the most dire consequences.

Until that time, my deepest condolences on your foolish action, and my best wishes for surviving the situation.

Sincerely,
S. H. Elives

Charlie stared at the letter for a long time. The old man had to be crazy. But if he was, then maybe craziness was catching. It was almost easier to believe that he himself had lost his mind than that he had just read a letter delivered by a pair of talking rats.

He glanced at the letter again and wondered if the rats had known what it said. Probably not, or they would have asked why the skull wasn't in his room.

Charlie felt a sudden sinking feeling in the pit of his stomach.

Under no circumstances should you let the skull out of your possession!

Was leaving it in the garage letting it out of his possession?

He had an uneasy feeling he should go get the thing.

He shuddered. Going to the garage attic in the middle of the night to retrieve a skull was the last thing in the world he wanted to do. But what if he didn't go get it, and in the morning it was gone? Would the old man have him arrested for being a thief if he couldn't return the skull when Mr. Elives came back and asked for it?

Charlie reread the letter, studying every word. The more he thought about it, the more he was sure that leaving the skull in the garage was a bad idea.

Grumbling to himself, he slipped into his clothes, then tiptoed down to the kitchen. Trying not to make too much noise, he dug a flashlight out of the tool drawer. Stewbone, curled up on his bed in the corner, whined in his sleep.

Charlie opened the back door of the house as quietly as he could and stepped onto the porch. The night was cool, the air crisp, the half moon bright enough that he didn't need the flashlight until he reached the garage. Dew glistened on the grass, and a chorus of spring peepers singing in the cemetery made him think of the swamp.

Slipping through the garage's side door, Charlie flicked on his flashlight, then retraced his steps from earlier in the evening. At the back of the garage he climbed the shaky wooden ladder to the attic.

The peak of the low ceiling was only a foot or two above his head. The cramped space was filled with several decades of family debris. Cobwebs stretched from rafter to rafter. A square of pale moonlight—the back window—was crisscrossed with dark lines made by the branches of the ancient apple tree that grew behind the building. Charlie could hear a scuttering and a scratching in the corners. Hoping the sound came from squirrels and not more rats, he began to pick his way along the floor.

Finally he came to the skull. It sat on an old brass-bound trunk, right where he had left it. Playing his light over it, he again felt shivery at the sight of its yellowing ivory dome and empty eye sockets—and more shivery still as he remembered the weird way in which he had ended up with the thing. He truly had *not* meant to take it out of the shop.

"What is this all about?" he said aloud.

He didn't really expect an answer, of course. So when a dim yellow light began to glow in the skull's eye sockets and it started to speak to him, it was all Charlie could do to keep from screaming.

FOUR

Truth to Tell

The voice was masculine but surprisingly high and light. It clearly came from the skull, even though there was no actual sound. It was as if the words were flowing directly into Charlie's brain.

"Look, I'd been in that shop forever! I was dying to get out." The skull paused, then shrieked: "*Dying to get out!* That's pretty good!"

It began to laugh hysterically.

Charlie was too terrified to join in the skull's merriment. Dropping the flashlight, he clutched his head, as if to drive out the intruding voice.

"What's the matter?" the skull asked.

With a squeak (he wanted to scream, but couldn't get one out) Charlie turned and began to stumble toward the ladder.

"You get back here right this instant, young man!"

Now Charlie did scream. He tried to move even faster, with the result that he tripped over a pair of old skis and went crashing into a pile of cardboard boxes. The boxes tumbled to the floor, with Charlie sprawled on top of them.

"For heaven's sake, settle down!" ordered the skull. "I won't hurt you."

"I don't believe you!" He was creeping toward the ladder now, moving backward so he could keep his eyes on the skull.

"That's pretty funny," snickered the grisly relic, "given the fact that I couldn't tell a lie if my life depended on it." After a fraction of a second it shrieked, "*If my life depended on it!* Oh, god—I kill me!"

The thought of not being able to tell a lie was so startling that Charlie actually stopped moving. "What do you mean?"

"Just what I said. I cannot tell a lie, even if I try. Dee dee-dee dee-dee, die dee-die dee-die."

Charlie shook his head. "I never thought a dead person would find things so funny."

"You think if I start to cry it will bring me back to life?"

Charlie felt himself redden, then got angry at being embarrassed by the skull. "Of course not! I just figured being dead was...was..." His voice trailed off, since he wasn't sure *what* he thought about it.

"Well, it ain't no picnic. But then, being alive wasn't that easy, either."

"You can say that again," muttered Charlie.

"Nah, you heard me the first time. Speaking of heard, did you hear the one about—"

"Oh, stop it! I'm in no mood for jokes!"

"Bad sign. Do you have a fever?"

"I'm not sick, I'm scared!"

"Of what? Me? Forget it. I wouldn't hurt a fly. No, that's not true. I hate flies. Always buzzing around me, creeping into my eye sockets. Man, I hate it when they get inside and crawl around. Tickles like crazy. I'd swat them in an instant if I still had hands. But I wouldn't hurt *you*, not after the favor you did me today!"

"What favor?"

"Getting me out of Elives' shop."

"How did that happen, anyway?" asked Charlie suspiciously.

"It was fate."

"Fate, my foot! I had no intention of stealing you from that shop."

"I think *liberating* would be a better word," said the skull primly. "I wanted a way out, and you provided it. Didn't you feel the electricity between us when you looked into my eyes and asked me that question?"

"What question?"

"*What* question? You said, and I quote, 'Want to come home with me?' I remember it distinctly. You mean you didn't really mean it? Gad, I'm crushed. Oh, well. You shouldn't ask if you're not interested. But that's what opened the lines of communication: you staring into my eyes—well, my eye sockets—and asking me a question."

Charlie shivered. "Can I go now?"

"You are planning on taking me with you, aren't you?"

"Well, actually—"

"I wouldn't risk the wrath of Elives if I were you, buddy. The old guy can be pretty tough."

Charlie sighed. "How long are you planning to stay?"

"How would I know?" Charlie could almost hear the shrug in the skull's voice. "As long as it takes, I guess."

"As long as *what* takes?"

"Whatever is supposed to happen."

"What are you talking about? What's supposed to happen?"

"I don't have the slightest idea," said the skull impatiently. "Life is mysterious." It paused, then added, "Death, too, for that matter."

With the skull tucked under one arm and the flashlight clenched between his teeth, Charlie climbed back down the ladder.

"This is going to be fun," the skull said as Charlie reached the last rung. "I haven't had a boy to hang around with since Hamlet was a pup. I bet you'll have fun, too, as long as—"

It broke off, as if it had said too much.

"As long as what?" asked Charlie nervously.

"Oh, nothing," said the skull airily. "Nothing at all."

Charlie was suspicious, but too tired to argue.

"Look at that moon!" cried the skull when they left the garage. "Oh, it *has* been too long since I've seen the moon."

Charlie looked up. With the ragged scraps of

cloud crossing its surface, the moon really was beautiful. However, it also looked mysterious, and somewhat frightening.

Shivering, he continued toward the house.

"The closet?" cried the skull, once Charlie was back in his room. "You're going to put me in the *closet?*"

"Well, if I leave you on my desk, I'm going to have to explain you to my mother. Does that sound like a good idea?"

After he asked the question, he was half afraid the skull would say yes. After all, just because *he* thought it was a bad idea didn't mean the skull would. But it sighed and said, "Oh, I suppose you've got a point. All right, the closet it is. Sheesh. Some grand return to the world this is."

Being careful, so as not to chip it, Charlie placed the skull between a stack of games and an old box of Legos on the top shelf.

Then he went to wash his hands.

Though Charlie was exhausted, he didn't sleep much. Every time he started to nod off, the memory of carrying the skull into the house and hiding it in his closet would drift to the surface and snap him back to wakefulness. Thank goodness that horrible yellow glow in its eyes had faded once it stopped talking to him!

He stared into the darkness, questions about the skull swirling through his mind. The problem was, the only way to get the answers was to talk to the thing, which was (a) terrifying, and (b) relatively useless, since the questions he *had* asked had gotten mostly wisecracks in response.

"Morning, Charlie," said Mimi, when he dragged himself down to breakfast the next day. "I dreamed I was a monkey. What did you dream?"

"I don't want to talk about it," he said, with absolute truthfulness.

His mother came to the table with a stack of toast. "You look horrible," she said, sounding worried. "Didn't you sleep well?"

Charlie shook his head.

"I'm sorry, sweetheart." Suddenly she got a suspicious look in her eyes. "Did you get your homework done?"

The question, which she actually asked every morning, was little more than a ritual. Charlie always claimed his work was done, whether it was or not, and they both knew it. So when he said, "No, I completely forgot about it," it would have been hard to say who was more astonished, Charlie or his mother.

After sitting for a moment with his spoon poised halfway between his cereal bowl and his mouth, he bolted from the table and raced up the stairs. Yanking open his closet door, he hissed, "Do you know what just happened to me?"

The skull's hollow eyes glowed into life. "Now, how would I know that?" it asked, the words forming inside Charlie's head.

"I don't know how! How come your eyes light up? How come you can talk directly into my brain?"

"I'm special."

"Well, then, maybe you're special enough to know what just happened downstairs."

"Sorry. I'm special, but not that special. So what did happen?"

"I just told my mother the truth!"

"What's so horrible about that?"

"I wasn't going to! I didn't want to! I just opened my mouth and out it came!"

"Uh-oh," said the skull. "I guess it's still working."

"What's still working?"

"The curse."

"*What curse?*"

The skull sighed. "The curse of truth. It's this thing that happened to me a while ago. I sort of... uh... force you to tell the truth."

"You *what*?"

"Oh, calm down. It won't hurt you to tell the truth for a while."

"Hurt me? Something like that could *kill* me!"

They were interrupted by his mother knocking at the door. "Charlie!" she called. "Charlie, are you all right?"

When he opened his mouth to answer her, he meant to say "I'm fine, I'll be right down." What actually came out was "No, I'm not all right. I'm very upset!"

He clapped his hand over his lips and glared at the skull.

The concern in his mother's voice grew deeper. "What's the matter, honey? Can I help you?"

Choosing his words carefully, Charlie replied, "It's something I have to take care of myself. I'll be down as soon as I can."

"All right. But don't be long. I don't want you to be late for school."

Normally he would have said, "Don't worry, I'll be on time." This morning he found that the words would not pass his lips. "I'll be there as soon as I can," he replied at last.

His mother stayed at the door a moment longer, then turned and went back downstairs.

"See what I mean?" he hissed at the skull. "I'm in trouble already!"

"Well, what do you want me to do about it? Anyway, there was nothing wrong with that conversation."

"Oh, forget it," he said, snatching up his backpack. "I gotta go."

"Take me with you."

He snorted. "Are you kidding?"

The skull's eyes glowed more brightly. "Hard to tell with me, isn't it?"

"I can't take you. I have nowhere to hide you, and no way to explain you."

"Suit yourself. I just thought you might like to have me along for the benefit of my wisdom."

"Hah!"

It was, without doubt, the worst day of Charlie's life—a three-act catastrophe that left him wondering if the appalling idea of bringing the skull with him might actually have saved him from his now compulsively truthful tongue.

Act 1 took place before school even started, when Mark Evans caught him on the playground while they were waiting for the doors to open.

"You're a liar, Charlie!" he said.

"That's not entirely accurate," replied Charlie— quite truthfully, given the morning's events.

"You lied about my father's project!"

"Only because I love Tucker's Swamp and your father wants to destroy it."

That would have been enough. It might even have held Mark off. But now that his mouth was in gear Charlie didn't seem to be able to stop himself, so he added something he had first heard from Uncle Bennie, and that he fervently believed to be true. "Your father's a nature-destroying capitalist swine."

That was when Mark knocked him down. Then he sat on Charlie, crying and pounding at his face, until the school principal, Mrs. Verna Lincoln, dragged him off.

Act 2 took place in the classroom and was humiliating in a much deeper way than the playground battle had been.

It started at 9:45, with the return of Gilbert

Dawkins, who had not been to school for three months—a fact that had been the cause of considerable gossip and guesswork. During that time Mr. Diogen would say only that Gilbert was sick; he had refused to offer any further details.

This morning he announced that Gilbert was returning.

And he would be completely bald.

"It's a side effect of his treatment. Naturally, I expect that none of you will tease him about it."

And Charlie wouldn't have, either. But Gilbert, with whom he had once been fairly friendly, made the mistake of asking Charlie what he thought. The idea, of course, was that Charlie would assure Gilbert that he looked okay, maybe even say that it was kind of cool. But faced with a direct question, Charlie had no choice but to respond with exactly what was on his mind.

"I think it looks totally doofy," he said. "And I hope to god it never happens to me."

The lecture he got from Mr. Diogen was the longest and most horrible he had ever received. The fact that he agreed with everything the teacher said didn't make it any easier to take.

Act 3 was brief, a ghastly climax to a terrible day. If it were possible to die of embarrassment, the event would probably have been fatal.

Like Act 1, it took place on the playground.

The class, most of which was officially not speaking to Charlie because of the Gilbert incident, had gone outside for recess. Feeling hurt and lonely, Charlie was delighted when Karen Ackerman, who had shimmering chestnut hair, an upturned nose, and the best batting average in the sixth grade, broke with popular opinion and came over to talk to him.

Unfortunately, what she came over to say was "I can't believe what you did this morning, Charlie. I always thought you were one of the nicest kids in the class, even if you do lie all the time. But you're the worst bully that I ever met."

She turned to go.

Desperate—too desperate to think straight— Charlie called, "Karen, wait! Please, *please* don't be mad at me!"

"Why not?" she asked, her voice dripping with contempt.

Before he could stop himself, Charlie replied. Opening his mouth, he gave Karen the most horrifying answer imaginable.

FIVE

The Truth Hurts

Two hours after the catastrophe on the playground, Charlie raced up the back steps of his house. Shooting through the kitchen, he ignored his mother, who was baking, and Mimi, who was finger painting. Jumping over Stewbone, he hit the stairs at a run, pounded up them, burst into his room, yanked open the closet door, and shouted, *"Do you know what happened to me today?"*

The skull's eyes began to glow. "Is this a game? Do I get a prize if I guess the right answer?"

"I'm serious!"

"Oh." It sounded disappointed. "Well, then, the answer is, 'No, I don't know what happened to you today.' "

"I told Karen Ackerman I love her! I opened my stupid fat mouth right there on the playground and said, 'Please, *please* don't be mad at me.' And when Karen asked why not, I opened it again and said, 'Because I love you!' "

He was silent for a moment, remembering the horror that had overwhelmed him when he realized what he had done. If he'd had the ability at that moment, he would gladly have dug a hole, climbed in, and pulled the dirt on top of himself.

Karen had said nothing, for she had been as shocked as he was. But her best friend, Loud Beth, had stood there shrieking with delight: "Charlie loves you! Karen, Charlie *loves* you!"

Charlie glared at the skull. "My life is over, and it's all your fault! I could kill you!"

"Sorry, somebody beat you to it."

Before Charlie could ask what the skull meant, he heard his mother. She was standing at the door to his room, looking worried. "Charlie, are you all right?"

He turned to face her, closing the closet door slightly to keep the skull hidden. "No, I am *not* all right."

"Do you want to talk about it?"

"No!"

Which was the absolute truth. He didn't want anyone else to know about his incredible humiliation. The only reason he was telling the skull about it was that he blamed the wretched thing for the entire mess.

His mother sighed. "You know, Charlie, sometimes things are better if you talk about them."

"Not this thing."

Mrs. Eggleston looked at her son a moment longer. "All right. But if you do decide you want to talk—"

She was interrupted by a wail from Mimi. "Momma! Momma! Come quick! I spilled again!"

Mrs. Eggleston rolled her eyes. "You know where to find me," she said, before she dashed away to deal with whatever disaster her youngest had just created.

Charlie turned back to the skull. "What would happen if I told my mother about you?"

The glow in the skull's eyes grew brighter. "Well, let's think about that. To begin with, she probably wouldn't believe you—which would be ironic, since you can't help but tell her the truth. So maybe nothing would happen except that she would be a little annoyed with you. If you persisted until you actually got her to come look at me, or if you took me down to show her, she would probably be appalled and insist that you get rid of me. Boy, would you be in trouble with Elives then! If you tried to explain *why* you had to keep me—told her the whole story about how you got me—she would probably decide you were losing your mind and take you to get professional help. Of course, since you can only speak the truth, you would keep telling the therapist the same story over and over again, which would lead him to decide you were hopelessly delusional.

"Bad events would likely follow.

"So-o-o-o . . . if you want my advice—don't do it."

Charlie sighed. He had worked out the same line of reasoning himself on the way home. He had been hoping the skull would say something different. "What if you talked to her?" he asked, though he wasn't actually sure this was a good idea. "She'd have to believe me then."

"That would probably convince her. But you'd have to get her to look in my eye sockets and ask me a direct question before I could do it."

Charlie groaned as he imagined trying to get his mother to ask the skull a question. With the curse on him, he would have to tell her the truth when she asked why he wanted her to do it. And given his reputation for making up stories, there was no way she would believe him when he told her. So the only way he could get her to discover the truth would be by lying to her—which was absolutely beyond his power right now.

"What am I going to do?" he moaned.

"Relax and enjoy the experience, baby."

Charlie wondered if breaking open a dead man's skull could be considered murder.

The horrible day had been a Friday, leaving Charlie to face a weekend of bitter regret whenever he thought about what he had done; total confusion when he tried to figure out how to patch things up with Gilbert; and intense fear whenever he thought about returning to school on Monday.

To make things worse, the skull kept him awake most of Friday night with a nonstop string of jokes, riddles, and songs.

"Don't you ever shut up?" asked Charlie wearily, at about three in the morning.

"I'm making up for lost time! It's been *years* since I've had someone new to talk to."

By the time Uncle Bennie called on Saturday afternoon to ask if Charlie wanted to go to a storytelling concert that night, Charlie was ready to jump at the offer as eagerly as if he had just been shown an escape route from a burning building—which, indeed, his mind was starting to resemble.

Bennie's roommate, Dave, was coming along, too. This was fine with Charlie. Dave was funny and weird, and seemed to know cool things—what movies were going to be really hot, for example—a month in advance of everyone else. Charlie had used Dave's information to good advantage in the past. If he was lucky, he would pick up some interesting tidbits that might help him climb out of the pit he had dug for himself at school.

That was assuming he ever went back again, an event he was trying to figure out how to avoid. . . .

"Take me with you," said the skull, when it saw Charlie dressing to go.

"Yeah, right. I'll get Uncle Bennie to buy a separate ticket, so you can have your own seat."

"Hey, you never know. You may need my advice. Remember what happened the last time you left the house without me!"

"The only advice I need is in Mr. Elives' letter," replied Charlie, who had decided the old man's words about being careful what he said and to whom he said it (not to mention the bit about not talking at all) were the wisest things he had ever read. If only the letter hadn't also insisted he had to take good care of the skull until Mr. Elives came back to get it!

"The old man wrote to you? What did he say?"

"It's private," replied Charlie, with some satisfaction.

"Take me with you," said the skull again, when Charlie was about to go out the door.

"I can't! Besides, I need a break from your chatter."

"I'm afraid to stay here alone!"

Charlie snorted. "What do *you* have to be afraid of? You're already dead!"

"Oh, getting personal, huh? Well, if you think being dead is the worst thing that can happen to you, you have a lot to learn, kid." Suddenly the skull's voice grew serious. "Listen, Charlie. Something's coming. I can feel it in my bones, if you know what I mean. It's like a storm just over the horizon, fierce and powerful but still out of sight. Only it's moving toward us and I don't want to stay here by myself."

Charlie shivered. The skull seemed so sincere that he wondered if he should take it seriously. What would happen if he came home and found it was gone? *Stolen.* What would Mr. Elives do to him then?

"Are you just making this up?" he asked suspiciously.

"As if! Don't you get it, Charlie? *I* can't lie, either."

"How do I know *that's* true?"

The skull sighed. "You'll have to take my word for it."

Sighing himself, Charlie got his backpack and

put the skull inside. Then he rolled up a couple of T-shirts and tucked them around the skull as padding, so it wouldn't chip or break. "You'd just better be quiet!" he said fiercely as he pulled the drawstrings that closed the top.

"Why? You're the only one who can hear me!"

"Lucky me. But I want to listen to the stories, not your chatter. All right?"

"Sure. I'll listen, too. I love stories."

"What's in the backpack, ace?" asked Uncle Bennie, when Charlie climbed into the backseat of his old convertible.

"The Skull of Truth," said Charlie, his stomach clenching nervously.

Dave laughed. "Boy, I can tell you two are from the same family, Bennie. He's as weird as you are!"

"Take that as a compliment," said Bennie, glancing at Charlie over his shoulder. Then they zoomed away from the curb, and the question of the backpack was dropped.

The storytelling concert was at the Tucker's Grove library, which had a small theater in the basement. Following Bennie and Dave down the stairs, Charlie wondered with a sudden thrill of horror if anyone else from his class would be there.

The reality was even worse. Though no one from his class was there, Gilbert's *mother* was, and the look she shot Charlie when she saw him chilled him to his very core.

The houselights began to dim. Charlie sat down and put the backpack in his lap.

The librarian, Mrs. Hayes, stepped onstage to introduce the storyteller. At least, Charlie hoped she was going to introduce the storyteller; she started with a list of thank-yous that Charlie feared might go on forever. But at last she said, "Ladies and gentlemen, please welcome our guest for the evening, our new children's librarian, Hyacinth Priest."

"That's my teacher," Bennie whispered proudly in Charlie's ear as the storyteller came out. Her flowing clothes were simple but elegant; her dangling earrings seemed to catch and play with the light— as did her enormous eyes. Standing in the center of the stage, she began to speak in a voice that was deep, rich, and clear.

Though the stage was tiny, it soon felt as wide as the wide, wide world to Charlie, for Ms. Priest swept him up and carried him away on the wings of her words. The experience had as much magic, he later thought, as anything you might find in Mr. Elives' shop. In fact, she was so compelling that even the skull stayed quiet during the performance—something Charlie had not expected it to do, despite its promise.

After the concert was over Bennie said, "I want to say hello to Hyacinth. Would you like to meet her, Charlie?"

Delighted, and a little nervous, Charlie nodded.

"No need to worry," said the skull, in words only Charlie could hear. "You can't embarrass yourself any more than you already have today."

As they stepped into the aisle, Mrs. Dawkins approached. Charlie braced himself for a tongue-lashing. But she simply held out a piece of folded paper and said, "Take this."

Charlie did as she told him. Before he could think of what to say (which might have taken all evening, because what was there to say under the circumstances?), she turned and walked away.

"Whew," said Dave with a low whistle. "That is *not* a happy lady. What'd you do, Charlie? Pee in her petunias?"

"I hurt her son's feelings," he replied, no longer surprised by his unavoidable forthrightness, simply relieved that he didn't feel compelled to go into the excruciating details.

His uncle looked startled.

"I didn't mean to! It was an...accident."

"Ah," said Bennie with a nod. "I know what you mean; happens to me all the time."

Charlie looked at him in surprise. But he wasn't able to ask about it because Bennie had turned and started down the aisle.

"Come on," said Dave. "He's in a hurry to make points with Ms. Priest. I think he has a crush on her."

Hyacinth Priest was talking with Mrs. Hayes and two other women when Bennie approached. She interrupted the conversation to greet him, seeming genuinely happy to see him, and glad to meet Dave as well. But when she was introduced to Charlie, her expression turned serious. "Ah. I am very pleased to meet you," she said, smiling at him as if they somehow shared a secret. She extended her hand, which Charlie shook without much vigor, being both too awed and too puzzled to muster a real grip. "Perhaps you'll stop by and see me sometime," she added.

"What do you mean?"

"Well, as Mrs. Hayes said, I'm the new children's librarian. You do use the library, don't you?"

"Sometimes," he said truthfully. Then, feeling a desperate need to be completely honest, he added, "But not very often."

"We'll have to see if we can do something about that," said Ms. Priest with a smile. Then she turned back to his uncle, leaving Charlie to wonder what was going on.

When they pulled up in front of Charlie's house, Bennie turned to Dave and said, "Mind waiting in the car for a minute? I want to talk to Charlie."

"No problem," said Dave. "Night, Charlie."

"Night," said Charlie, wondering what his uncle wanted. Shouldering his backpack, he followed his uncle up the steps to the porch. The night was lovely, warm and dark. Instead of going inside, they sat on the porch swing. Its chain creaked gently as they moved back and forth, its sound melding with the peepers' singing in the distance. Charlie sat without speaking. Finally Bennie said, "Your mom told me you had a bad day at school yesterday. Want to talk about it?"

"No," said Charlie. At least, that was what he

meant to say. To his astonishment, what actually came out of his mouth was "Yes."

Charlie blinked. That couldn't be true—could it? But when he thought about it, he realized he did indeed want to talk about the whole mess; embarrassed and upset as he was, he was also in desperate need of advice. Choosing his words carefully, he gave Bennie an abbreviated account of what had happened the day before, managing to leave out any mention of the skull.

When he was done, Bennie shook his head and whistled. "So that's why Gilbert's Mom handed you that note tonight. Wow. I bet it's a scorcher. Man! I've had some bad days, but I think yours may take the cake. I'm impressed, buddy!"

"Thanks a lot! What am I going to *do* about it?"

Bennie smiled. "Well, it seems to me that this is a case where honesty is the best policy."

"It was honesty that got me into this!" cried Charlie, ignoring the snort of triumph the skull sent into his brain.

"And now you need some more of it to get out," replied Bennie calmly. "After all, you didn't *mean* to hurt Gilbert's feelings, did you?"

"Of course not."

"And you wish you hadn't done it?"

"You're not kidding!"

"So go to Gilbert and talk to him about it. Odds are everyone else was thinking pretty much what you said. You were just the one unlucky enough to blurt it out. Tell him you're sorry, and ask if he'll forgive you."

Charlie made a face.

Bennie laughed. "Yeah, it won't be easy. But one nasty scene, and it should all be over."

"And what about Karen?"

Bennie looked at him very seriously. "Love is nothing to be ashamed of, Charlie. That may be hard to believe at your age, but trust me—if we could all just be honest about love, everyone's lives would be a lot simpler. You should never let anyone make you feel bad for loving someone."

"Easy for you to say. You didn't blurt it out on the playground."

Bennie closed his eyes. "You do seem to be developing a gift for saying things at the most inopportune times, Charlie."

"I wouldn't exactly call it a gift."

"Whatever. Just try to remember what I said. It's important."

"Nice guy," said the skull, when they were back in Charlie's room. "I wonder what he's hiding."

"What do you mean?" asked Charlie, removing the skull from his backpack and taking it to the closet.

"Just what I said. He's keeping a secret of some kind. Trust me, kid; I know about these things."

Unable to think of a reply, Charlie ignored the skull and dug into his pants pocket for the note Mrs. Dawkins had given him. He stared at it for a moment, then crumpled it angrily and went to throw it away. But when he reached the basket, he couldn't bring himself to drop it in.

Taking a deep breath, he smoothed out the paper and went back to his desk to read it.

SIX

Jest in Time

The letter was written on a piece of lined yellow paper. Several places had been crossed out, including a long section at the end. The ink had run in a couple of spots; Charlie was pretty sure it was because Mrs. Dawkins had been crying as she wrote it.

It read as follows:

Dear Charlie,

I have always thought you were a nice boy. It used to please me when you came to the house to play with Gilbert—even if you did stretch the truth sometimes. So I was sad and surprised to find out what you said to Gilbert in school yesterday.

Perhaps you didn't realize how cruel you were being. I'm sure you don't know that when Gilbert came home he locked himself in his bedroom and cried for over an hour.

Charlie, during the last three months Gilbert

has had chemical treatments that made him so sick he could barely stand up. He lost all his hair, and nearly a quarter of his body weight. What he didn't lose was his sense of humor about it. It was only yesterday—after he'd gone to school and someone he had thought was his friend, someone he had missed very badly, said cruel things to him—that I finally saw it all get to him.

I thought about calling your parents but decided against it. But when I saw you here, I had to let you know how I felt. You see, Charlie, Gilbert was supposed to be here tonight, too. He had been looking forward to it for a long time. But when it was time to leave, I couldn't get him to come. He was too embarrassed—too afraid someone else would laugh at him.

Everything underneath that had been crossed out. Beneath all the scribbles the letter was signed, *Virginia Dawkins.*

"What does it say?" asked the skull.

"Never mind!"

He wanted to throw the letter away. But somehow he felt that he had to keep it until he managed to make things right again. Refolding the paper, he tucked it carefully into the back of his sock drawer.

His heart feeling as if it had turned to lead, Charlie got ready for bed.

Sleep wouldn't come. He tossed and turned until past midnight before he began to settle down. Just as he *was* finally drifting off, the skull said, "Knock knock."

Charlie didn't answer.

The skull repeated the words, more loudly this time.

"Who's there?" snapped Charlie, without opening his eyes.

"Isaiah."

Charlie groaned. "Isaiah who?"

"I zay a lot of stuff, but you don't pay attention. —Come on, Charlie. I wanna tell you some jokes."

"And I want to go to sleep!"

"Are you kidding? When you have me, the one and only Skull o' Truth (TM), to talk to? Say, did you hear the one about the guy who walked into a bar with a duck under his arm?"

"Be *quiet!*" hissed Charlie. He turned over and pressed his pillow against his ears.

Since the skull was speaking directly into his head, this did him no good. "Jeez," it said in a whiny voice, "you're no fun at all."

"I'm not surprised someone killed you!" Charlie snapped, flinging aside the pillow. "I'd consider it myself, if you weren't already dead!"

"You wouldn't talk like that if you knew how I died."

"How *did* you die?" asked Charlie, curious in spite of himself.

"Do you really want to know?"

"I'd love to," he said spitefully.

"Then come here."

"Why?"

"This will work better if you take me out of the closet."

"What will work better?"

"I'm going to show you what happened to me."

Charlie hesitated, then threw aside the covers and went to the closet. "I can't believe I'm doing this," he growled.

"We're all slaves to curiosity, bucko. Find someplace where you can be comfortable and put your hands on either side of me."

Charlie positioned the skull in the middle of his desk, then sat in front of it and placed his hands as the skull had directed.

"Not like *that*!" it said testily.

"What do you mean?"

"I mean, don't leave your hands lying on the desk like a pair of dead pigeons. When I said 'either side of me,' I meant *holding* me. But keep your thumbs out of my eye sockets. I hate it when that happens."

Gingerly Charlie placed his hands against the skull. The heel of each palm fit snugly in the ridge that ran beside the eye sockets. The curved dome felt smooth and cool.

"Ready?" asked the skull.

"I guess so."

"Then heeeeere we go!"

Charlie felt as if he were being spun about. The skull chuckled hollowly, the sound of its laugh reverberating through Charlie's head. A cold wind seemed to rush past.

Suddenly he gasped in astonishment. He was standing on a point of land that rose about twenty feet above a rocky coastline. Gray water smashed against the shore, sending a spray high enough that he could feel it. Thick clouds massed overhead, and a cold wind shrieked around him.

"Where am I?" he asked nervously.

"*You* are still in your room. This is just the setting for the story I want to tell you. Think of me as—oh, sort of as an internal television set."

"Television doesn't usually get me wet," replied Charlie, as the spray from another wave struck his legs.

"All right, so I'm a multimedia extravaganza. Call it Skull-o-Vision. Can we get on with the story?"

"Am I going to be cold and wet during the whole thing?"

The skull sighed, but the feeling of wetness vanished.

"Thanks."

"Don't mention it. Ever. Now, back this way is where I was born and raised."

Charlie found himself moving away from the coast. He wasn't walking; it felt more like he was watching one of those scenes in a film where the camera glides over the landscape. Only somehow he had become the camera. The countryside below had thick forests, and vast bogs that reminded him of Tucker's Swamp. But it seemed deserted, with only a scattering of huts and cottages.

"How come you can make me see all this?"

"Being dead does have a *few* compensations. Ah,

look! That's where I was born! And there's dear old Mom.''

They were hovering over a small stone hut. In front of it stood a woman dressed in garments made of fur. She was tall and coarse-looking. As Charlie watched, a boy of six or seven came bouncing through the door. He tugged at the woman's leggings. When she turned to him he lifted his leg and broke wind. Then he began to giggle.

"Me," said the skull proudly. "I was always looking for a laugh, even back then."

"Doesn't look like you got one," replied Charlie. Indeed, the tall woman had started to yell at the boy, who was now looking at the ground with teary eyes and quivering lip. Suddenly she lifted her hand and gave him a heavy clout.

"Mom didn't appreciate my sense of humor. That's one of the reasons I left so early."

"How old were you when you went?" asked Charlie, who had entertained visions of running away from home more than once in the last couple of days himself. "And where did you go?"

"I was fourteen. And I went on a quest for Truth."

When Charlie snorted, the skull replied, "Don't laugh. I was young and idealistic. Besides, I almost found her."

"Almost?" asked Charlie. And then, *"Her?"*

"Well, I think I got pretty close. I met this crazy old woman who claimed she knew where Truth lived. She told me if I apprenticed myself to her for a year and a day she would give me the directions. I had been there just one week short of a year when I blew it."

The scene shifted again, to a thatch-roofed hut in a forest clearing. In front of the hut crackled a greenish fire. Suspended above the fire was a large black cauldron filled with a thick concoction that bubbled and popped like the mud in the hot springs Charlie's family had seen in one of the national parks two summers earlier. To Charlie's surprise he could smell the stuff. It was disgusting—heavy, sweet, and rotting all at once.

A young man, probably in his late teens, stumbled into the clearing. He was fairly handsome, with a thick head of red hair. He carried an armload of wood, which he fed to the fire.

The cauldron began to bubble more intensely, causing its contents to slop over the sides. Whenever some of the stuff hit the flames, they shot up in brightly colored shafts.

An old woman hobbled out of the cottage, leaning on a stick. She wore a tattered gray dress. Her gray hair, long and matted, hung nearly to her waist. A large black cat lounged disdainfully across her shoulders.

Approaching the young man, the woman grabbed his chin with her gnarled hand. Turning his head so that he was looking directly into her face, she asked in a voice that sounded like a rusty hinge, "Do you think I'm ugly?"

The young man looked around desperately, as

if hoping someone else might answer the question.

"Do you think I'm ugly?" repeated the old woman, tightening her grip.

"Well, you aren't the queen of the May," said the young man, trying to smile.

He winced as her clawlike fingers clenched his jaw still tighter. "Do...you...think...I'm...*ugly*?"

The young man's eyes rolled to the side.

"Look at me!"

He turned his eyes full on her and whispered, "No, you're not ugly. In fact, you're really quite attractive!"

"Liar!" shrieked the old woman, her voice filled with despair. *"Liar!"* The cat leaped from her shoulder, hissing and spitting, and ran into the darkness.

To Charlie's horror, the woman dragged the young man to the cauldron. As he screamed and struggled, she thrust his head into the bubbling brew. "You longed for Truth!" she cried as lightning crackled in the sky above them. "Longed for it, but weren't brave enough to give it. Now be cursed with it!"

The boy's body jerked and twisted as he struggled to free himself. After a moment the old woman pulled his head from the cauldron. Charlie flinched, expecting to see the boy's face horribly scalded by the brew. Surprisingly, his skin was smooth and clear, seemingly unscathed. But his red hair had changed to purest white.

"From this day forth you shall speak nothing

except the truth," cried the old woman. "Little good may it do you!"

"And little good it *did* do me," said the skull, as Charlie watched the young man flee the clearing. "Cursed to speak only the truth, I couldn't go anywhere without offending *someone*. Oh, I'd make friends and get along for a while. But sooner or later someone would ask a question they didn't really want an answer to, and that would be the end of it."

"What kind of question?"

"Oh, you know: Did I like their cooking? Did I think their joke was funny? Did I agree that their daughter was beautiful? I would tell the truth, as the curse compelled me to, and end up being about as welcome as a booger in the butter. Finally I learned to cover some of the truth with jokes. As time went on, I got better and better at it.

"Eventually I found the perfect job for someone with my . . . problem."

As the skull said this, Charlie found himself rushing toward a gloomy-looking castle. It stood atop a rocky spit of land that thrust out into a cold-looking sea. Scarlet flags and pennons snapped from its towers, bright scars against the dark sky that loured behind it.

Before he could really study the place, they were inside, staring down at the throne room as if they had been somehow attached to the ceiling. The white-haired youth they had watched flee the witch's hut, now a young man, was dressed in jester's motley and crawling around on his hands and knees. On his back he carried a small boy. Shrieking with laughter, the child kicked his heels into the jester's side, shouting, "Faster! Faster!"

"Have mercy on your poor horse, my prince," gasped the jester as he scrambled across the floor. "I'm going as fast as I—well, actually I can go a *little* faster."

Kicking up his heels, he made three rapid circles in front of the thrones while the child on his back shrieked with delight.

"Alas, my poor fool," laughed the king. "I fear you shall never have rest till the prince is grown."

"I love you, horse!" cried the boy. Then he threw his arms around the fool's neck and kissed him.

"You were a court jester?" asked Charlie.

"Given my personality, it was a natural choice. Besides, the only people who can get away with telling the absolute truth are fools and poets. It's part of the job. And even then you have to be careful about it. I managed to pull it off here for nearly ten years—told the king all sorts of things he didn't really want to hear, but did it with a joke and a song, so he could either ignore them, or pretend it was just me being foolish."

The skull sighed. "Those were good years, overall. I cut some wild capers in those days, Charlie. Danced and frolicked and said the most outrageous things. But it couldn't last. The scene I'm showing you now is from my last night in the court. I might have made it longer, if there hadn't been something rotten in Denmark."

"I'm in Denmark?" asked Charlie in astonishment.

"No, you're in your room, just like I told you. But the things I'm showing you happened in Denmark, nearly a thousand years ago."

"What's the king's name?"

"Hamlet."

"Are you kidding? The 'To be or not to be' guy?"

"No, that would be the little git sitting on my back and turning my ribs black and blue. Hamlet Two, so to speak. Poor little guy; he was pretty happy back then. That was before everything started to turn sour. Broke his heart when he lost me. His father never did tell him the truth about that. He let the boy think I died in an accident."

"I take it you didn't."

"Not unless it was an accident when they threw me in the dungeon, beat me, and left me to starve."

Though the skull didn't show him the scene, in the back of his head Charlie heard the echo of an ancient scream, and then a muffled sobbing.

"I see," he said with a shudder.

"I doubt it," replied the skull. "At least, not entirely. But probably close enough for the spell to accept it as truth."

"What did you do to get thrown in the dungeon?"

"Queen Gertrude didn't like me."

"Because you told the truth?"

"Well, to be specific, I told the truth about *her*, which wasn't pretty. Anyway, that's how I died. Told one too many pieces of truth. It's dangerous stuff, as you know."

"So how did you end up in Mr. Elives' shop?"

A whirl of color exploded around them. "A little special effect to denote the passing of time," said the skull pleasantly. "Okay, we've jumped ahead by twenty-some years."

"I can't see a thing. Where are we?"

"Underground."

"What are we doing underground?"

"These are grave circumstances, Charlie," said the skull. Then it made a spooky laugh.

"Wait a minute...You don't mean—"

Charlie broke off as he was struck by an overwhelming sense of confinement and dampness. He felt as if he couldn't breathe, couldn't move.

A single thought burned in his brain. *I've been buried alive!*

He started to scream.

SEVEN

Grave
Circumstances

"Oh, calm down," said the skull. "You've only
been down here about ten seconds. I was moldering
underground for twenty-three *years*. And I'm not
even throwing in the really ooky stuff, like the
worms. You wanna talk special effects? Wowza! Anyway, you might as well face the truth: Once you're
dead they bury you—at least, they do if they don't
want you smelling the place up."

"So this is what happens after you die?" asked
Charlie in horror.

"Let's just say it's what happened to *me,* person-
ally, after *I* died. But you have to remember I had
been cursed by that old witch in the forest, so I was
not what you would call a typical case. I don't have
the slightest idea what happens to other people
when they take the big dirt nap. But I was definitely
stuck here. Oh, I did the ghost bit for a while; sort
of egged on old Hamlet One when he crossed the
line himself, which may or may not have been a good

idea. But my spirit could never get very far from the grave; tied too closely to my bones, I guess. Mostly I slept. Had really lousy dreams, too."

As the skull spoke a sudden shaft of light startled Charlie. From the sound that accompanied it, he realized it was caused by a spade thrusting through the soil above them. The spade pulled away, taking a clump of dirt with it. Charlie found himself looking up at smooth earthen walls, through which thrust crooked roots and the raw ends of worm-cleaned bones.

"Ah," said the skull. "It's morning in Denmark."

"How come someone's digging up your grave?"

"He's not digging up mine; he's digging a new one. It just happens to be in the same spot."

"That's disgusting!"

"Different times, different customs. Now stop chattering and pay attention."

The spade thrust down again. As it did, Charlie heard someone talking above them. Again and again the spade returned, until finally it lifted the skull from its resting place and tossed it toward the pile of dirt beside the grave.

As Charlie saw the world whirl above him he understood that he was actually seeing all this through the skull's eyes—or eye sockets, as the case might be. Suddenly its lower jaw fell off and went spinning in the other direction.

"I hated it when that happened," said the skull bitterly.

They landed on the pile of dirt. Moments later

the grave digger—who was standing *in* the grave—reached over and lifted the skull, raising it above him.

"Whose do you think it was?" he asked, speaking to someone Charlie couldn't see.

"Nay, I know not."

The grave digger turned the skull around, at which point Charlie was able to see two young men staring into the grave-in-progress. Both were noble-looking; one, dressed all in black, had a tragic air about him.

"My little buddy Hamlet Two, all grown up," whispered the skull. "I wish—"

He was interrupted by the grave digger shaking him. "A pestilence on him for a mad rogue! 'A poured a flagon of Rhenish on my head once. This same skull, sir, was, sir, Yorick's skull, the king's jester."

The man in black reached down and took the skull from the grave digger. "This?" he asked, his voice thick with horror and sorrow. With his finger-tips he tenderly brushed away a bit of dirt from the skull's left eye socket.

"E'en that," confirmed the grave digger.

"Alas, poor Yorick!" sighed Hamlet. He turned to his friend. "I knew him, Horatio—a fellow of infinite jest, of most excellent fancy. He hath bore me on his back a thousand times." Hamlet stared at the skull sadly, then pressed his finger to the ridge above the teeth. "Here hung those lips that I have kissed I know not how oft. Where be your gibes now, your

gambols, your songs, your flashes of merriment that were wont to set the table on a roar?"

Charlie half expected Yorick to answer the prince. When he remained silent Charlie asked him why.

"I hadn't figured out how to talk yet. Remember, this is a flashback. I hadn't been out of the ground more than two minutes when Hamlet started going on like that."

"Tell me, Horatio," continued the prince. "Dost think Alexander the Great looked like this once in the earth?"

"E'en so."

"And smelled so? Pah!" With that he tossed Yorick back onto the pile of dirt. But he continued his talk of death and what it meant until he heard the funeral procession approaching. Then Hamlet and his friend stepped back among the trees to watch in secret.

From their graveside spot, Charlie and Yorick had a perfect view of the action that followed.

First the body of a beautiful young woman all wrapped in white was lowered into the grave.

Then the queen—Charlie recognized her as Hamlet's mother, though she was quite a bit older now—threw flowers into the grave. "Sweets to the sweet," she whispered. "Farewell."

Then a young man jumped into the grave, crying, "Hold off the earth a while, till I have caught her once more in mine arms."

"Who's that?" asked Charlie.

"Her brother, Laertes," replied the skull. "Nice guy, but he tended to get a little carried away. On the other hand, so did Hamlet."

No sooner had Yorick said this than Hamlet came rushing out of the woods shouting, "*I* loved Ophelia! Forty thousand brothers could not with all their quality of love make up my sum."

Before long, he and Laertes were fighting about who was most upset by the girl's death.

Finally the fight was broken up and everyone left.

The skull was still lying out in the open.

"Boy, those guys really got carried away," said Charlie.

"They had very dysfunctional families," replied Yorick.

The grave digger began to shovel the dirt back into the hole, whistling cheerily as he covered the body that lay within. When the grave was about half full he thrust the shovel under the skull and lifted it. Then, as if thinking twice, he set the shovel down, picked up the skull, and put it off to the side.

Returning to his work, he soon had the grave filled.

"Why didn't he put you back?" asked Charlie.

"Pocket money." And indeed, after another "special effects" shift, Charlie was able to watch the grave digger carry the skull into a dark room. The man put the skull down, held out his hand, received a few tarnished coins, then went whistling into the dark.

"This was when I found out part two of the

curse," said the skull. "Now that I was dead, I not only had to speak the truth myself, I compelled it from others. You don't need the whole story, but believe me, no one wanted to keep me around for very long. I was extremely bad for business. So for centuries I passed from hand to hand, sometimes for money, more often not, given how badly people wanted to get rid of me. Finally I ended up with *this* guy..."

Another whirl of color, and Charlie found himself sitting on a table in a sparsely furnished room. He felt something warm above him and asked what it was.

"Wax. My new owner liked to use me as a candleholder."

As Charlie watched, a balding, bearded man sat down at the table, picked up a quill pen, and began to write.

"What's he working on?" asked Charlie.

"A play. *Hamlet,* to be precise."

"That isn't...?"

"Big Bill Shakespeare? Of course it is. Where do you think he got the story? This was a pretty happy time for me. Old Will loved having me around."

"Didn't you get him in trouble?"

"Oh, a little. But like fools, poets can be very good at telling the truth without getting into too much hot water for it. Besides, Will always said that what trouble I did cause was worth it for what I added to his poetry."

"You're not claiming you helped Shakespeare

write his plays, are you?" asked Charlie indignantly.

"Of course not. But as long as he had me around he couldn't write a line that wasn't true. I saved him from some real clinkers."

"Are you telling me everything in his plays actually happened?"

The skull sighed. "Truth comes in a lot of forms, Charlie. What I'm telling you is that everything he wrote after he got me was true in a way that few scriveners ever manage. True at the deepest level. I stayed with him till the very end...A few days after he was buried, someone came and bought me from his daughter."

As Yorick said this, Charlie saw a man who looked an awful lot like Mr. Elives pick up the skull and walk away with it. He thought about asking if it *was* Mr. Elives, decided the idea was absurd, then decided that given his current situation nothing was impossible.

"That's not the same old man I met in the magic shop, is it?" asked Charlie.

"I can't say," replied the skull.

Charlie had a feeling this was the absolute truth.

"What I *can* tell you is that from that day until the day you took me from the shop, I hadn't been out loose in the world."

"You seem to know a lot about the world for someone who's been locked away for almost four centuries," said Charlie, thinking of some of the jokes the skull had told him.

Yorick chuckled. "When you're dead you have

other ways to communicate, sort of a psychic version of the Internet. And I have to keep up with things for professional reasons. After all, a lot of humor is very topical. Best joke I ever knew was about Millard Fillmore. Screamingly funny. Unfortunately, I doubt one person in a million would understand it today."

"Who's Millard Fillmore?"

"You make my point perfectly."

Charlie realized that the story was over, that he was once more aware of his room. "So how come you chose *me* to take you out of the shop?" he asked.

"I keep telling you, *you* chose *me*. Looked right into my big empty eye sockets and asked me if I wanted to come home with you. I was restless, so I took advantage of the situation and sort of urged you to pick me up. I hope you don't mind."

It was easy to respond truthfully: "I do."

The skull sighed. "You lack a sense of adventure."

"You lack a sense of decency," shot back Charlie.

"Oh yeah? Well you lack a sense of...of...oh, drat. I guess you don't."

"What? What were you going to say?"

"That you lacked a sense of humor, but I couldn't get the words out. So must be it's not true."

"Heh. Just because I don't laugh at *your* jokes doesn't mean I don't have a sense of humor," said Charlie smugly.

"Oh, that was low," said the skull. "And I could say that, so you can see it must be true."

Charlie collapsed onto his bed. "Oh, it's true all

right." He sighed. "I am low. Only a low, vile, rotten human being could do what I did to Gilbert yesterday." He groaned. "Oh, god. I thought I was exaggerating! Must be I *am* low, vile, and rotten!"

The skull began to laugh.

"I don't see what's so funny!" snarled Charlie.

"Okay, then try saying this: 'Only a fine, sensitive human being would worry so much about how Gilbert feels.' "

Charlie repeated the sentence. His eyes widened. "Did something break the spell?"

"Of course not."

"Then I don't get it. Supposedly I can only say what's true. So which is it? Am I low, vile, and rotten—or fine and sensitive?"

"Both, just like most human beings."

Charlie made a face. "That's the silliest thing I ever heard."

"Hey, just because I only tell the truth doesn't mean I have to make sense. Half of what I say is stranger than fiction. But it's all true. Guaranteed."

When Charlie woke the next morning he was surprised to find his mother and sisters had already gone to church. His father was sitting in the living room, reading the funnies.

"Morning, champ," he said as Charlie stumbled down the stairs. "We decided to let you sleep in today."

"Thanks," said Charlie, using his fingers to comb some of the knots out of his hair.

Mr. Eggleston shrugged. "To tell you the truth, it made a good excuse for me to stay home myself." He looked startled, then said gruffly, "There's bagels in the kitchen."

Charlie looked at his father oddly, then went to get some breakfast. Afterward he rode his bike to Tucker's Swamp and sat staring at the water for a long time.

When he returned to his room Charlie noticed that Yorick was unusually quiet. Though he welcomed the silence, after about half an hour it began to get on his nerves. He wondered if the skull was angry at him.

Finally he went to the closet and opened the door.

"Why are you being so quiet, Yorick?"

The skull didn't reply for so long that Charlie wondered if it was going to refuse to answer altogether. He was considering just leaving the room when Yorick said, very softly, "I'm scared."

Charlie blinked. "Why?"

"I told you last night: *Something* is coming. I don't know what. I don't know when. But whatever it is, it scares me. If I had a body, I'd shiver."

Charlie did shiver. The first time the skull had talked this way, Charlie had told himself it was probably joking, since that seemed to be all it did anyway. But now that he knew the skull's story, he wasn't so sure. Besides, the fear in Yorick's voice *felt* genuine.

"Maybe we'd better stick together," said Charlie,

somewhat reluctantly. He was about to ask the skull if it had any advice for dealing with the Gilbert situation when Mimi appeared at his door and said, "Mommy wants to talk to you."

Shifting to make sure he kept the skull hidden from her sight, he turned to face her. "What does she want?"

Mimi shrugged and took a bite of her cookie. "I dunno."

Charlie sighed. "Well, did she sound mad?"

"I dunno. She's in her workshop."

"Tell her I'll be right there."

"Okey-padokey!"

He waited until Mimi had headed down the hall, then turned back to Yorick. "I'll see you in a while," he said. Then he closed the closet door and headed for the garage.

His mother was on her knees, stripping green paint off an old kitchen chair. Scuds of it lay curled on the newspapers she had spread underneath the project. The wood she had revealed looked fresh and clean. A sharp chemical smell lingered in the air.

"Mimi said you wanted to see me."

"I heard something at church this morning," said Mrs. Eggleston softly, not looking up. She slid her blade under some paint, lifting it away from the wood. "Something that upset me a great deal."

He felt his stomach begin to knot up. "What was it?" he asked, trying to sound casual.

"It was about you, Charlie. Do you know what it was?"

Offhand, he could think of several things his mother might have heard about him that would upset her. But odds were good that the current item had to do with what had happened on Friday.

"Was it about Gilbert Dawkins?" His voice came out tinier than he had meant it to.

His mother set aside her scraper and stood up. When she turned to him, her eyes were sad. "Oh, Charlie," she whispered. *"How could you?"*

To Charlie's surprise, he started to cry. He didn't say anything, just ran to her and threw his arms around her and buried his face against her like he used to do when he was little. Gasping sobs shook his body. When he could finally speak he said, "I didn't mean to. I didn't mean to. It just came out. And now everyone hates me!"

She held him close and patted his back. "Oh, sweetheart. They don't hate you." Then, sounding slightly uncomfortable, she added, "But they probably don't like you much right now."

"What can I do?" whispered Charlie, too upset at first to realize what was happening.

His mother thought for a moment. "You'll have to see if you can make it up to Gilbert somehow. Have you apologized yet?"

Charlie shook his head. "I was afraid to. Besides, I feel so stupid."

"Don't," said his mother gently. She ruffled his hair. "We all make mistakes, honey. It happens. I think you should call Gil right away, so you can try to get things settled before you have to go back to school tomorrow."

Charlie sighed. "You're probably right."

He turned to go. As he did, his mother said, "By the way, I've been meaning to remind you we're having a family dinner to celebrate Gramma Ethel's birthday tonight. Please don't be late this time. And please have *something* to give her. It doesn't have to be much. Just a card would be fine."

Charlie sighed again, more heavily this time. "Do we have to have so many family dinners? I'm getting tired of them."

"Well how do you think *I* feel?" snapped his mother. "They're important for the family, but the truth is they're a real pain in the butt for me!"

Her eyes grew wide and she pulled her head back in astonishment. "Charlie, I'm sorry! I didn't mean to say that!"

Charlie nodded. He believed her.

In fact, he had no question at all that she was telling the absolute truth.

EIGHT

A Promise,
a Warning, a Shrug

"It's getting worse!" said Charlie, when he was safely back in his room.

"What's getting worse?" asked Yorick, his eye sockets starting to glow. "Your haircut? Your breath? Your grade-point average?"

"Your jokes," replied Charlie sharply. Then he smiled. "Heh. Must be *that's* true." His moment of triumph was short-lived, as he remembered what had happened downstairs. "But that's not what I'm talking about. It's the curse; it's spreading. *I think my mom is catching it!*"

"Uh-oh. This could be serious."

"What do you mean? My mother always tells the truth anyway."

"Are you kidding? If mothers started telling the absolute truth it would mean the end of life as you know it. Besides, if your mom always tells the truth, then what makes you think the curse is affecting her?"

The phone rang, interrupting Charlie's fumbling attempts to come up with an answer.

"Charlie!" cried Tiffany. "It's for you! It's Karen." She made a series of kissing sounds, then began to giggle.

"Saved by the bell," muttered Yorick, as Charlie hurried to take the call.

When Charlie picked up the receiver he found that his voice was so weak the words could barely pass his lips. "Hi," he said, after two or three tries. "I thought you weren't speaking to me."

"I'm not," replied Karen. "I only called to find out what you were going to do to patch things up with Gilbert."

"I don't know," said Charlie miserably. Then, when there was silence on the other end of the line, he added in a rush, "But I'm going to do *something*! I can't tell you how rotten I feel. Well, actually, I can. I feel like a two-pound ball of slug slime that's been sitting in a closed container and turning—"

"Oh, stop! I get the idea. And I believe you. But I don't feel sorry for you. You *should* feel rotten."

"Do you have any suggestions?" asked Charlie.

Karen paused. "No. I just wanted to make sure you were going to do *something*."

"I will. Right away. I promise."

Charlie knew Karen would believe that. Even though he always lied about things—or used to, before the skull came along—promises were sacred as far as he was concerned. The other kids had reached the point where they never believed anything he said without a promise; with a promise, they were willing to trust him completely.

"All right," said Karen. "I'll see you tomorrow."

She hung up. Charlie put down the receiver, a broad grin creasing his face. *She likes me!* he thought. Then he realized with horror what he had just promised to do.

When Charlie returned to his room, his brooding about how to handle the Gilbert situation was interrupted by Yorick saying, "We've got company."

"What are you talking about?" asked Charlie. Then he jumped as a rat came scurrying out from under his desk.

"Surprise!" it cried, standing on its hind legs.

"Jerome! What are you doing here?"

"Don't be so rude, Charlie," said Roxanne, coming out to stand beside Jerome. "You could have said 'Nice to see you.' Or 'Well, what a surprise! How are you, Jerome?' Or something like that. Any of a number of things would have been more pleasant than 'What are *you* doing here?' Hasn't your mother taught you any manners?"

"She keeps trying. Anyway, I'm not sure it *is* nice to see you. You kind of scare me."

"Well, you scare me," said Jerome. "But the old man wanted us to bring you another message."

"How did you get in?" asked Charlie, glancing at the window and seeing that it was still closed.

"Rats are very good at getting into places," said Roxanne. "It's one of the things that make us such good messengers. First time, we couldn't come in until you had invited us. That's one of the rules. But now it's easier.''

"Great," muttered Charlie, wondering if he was going to be seeing the rats on a regular basis, and at the same time noticing that the truth spell didn't inhibit sarcasm.

"Here's the message," said Jerome, dragging a rolled-up piece of paper from under the desk.

"Sign here," added Roxanne, producing a receipt.

Charlie read it to make sure he wasn't signing anything dangerous, then scrawled his name.

Jerome handed him the message. "Good luck," said the rat darkly. Then he and Roxanne headed back under the desk. A second later Roxanne scurried back and said, "It was nice to see you again, Yorick. It's kind of quiet around the shop without you." Dropping her voice to a whisper, she added, "No offense, but I think Jerome is glad you're gone."

"Why?" asked Yorick, sounding deeply offended anyway.

Roxanne glanced over her shoulder, then turned back and whispered, "You're funnier than he is. It depresses him." With a little giggle she scooted under the desk.

Charlie dropped to his knees and peered after Roxanne. She and Jerome had both vanished, and he could see no sign of where they had gone. Sighing, he got to his feet, then went to his desk and unrolled the message.

To: Charlie Eggleston
From: S. H. Elives
Regarding: Warning Signs

Mr. Eggleston,

Signs indicate that you are entering a time of great danger. I have word of something that lurches toward you, something that wants the skull. The threads of truth are tangled around poor Yorick in ways I cannot yet determine.

That you are in the center of this, while only partly your fault, is definitely your problem. I regret I am not able to return at this time. However, I will send help and advice as I am able. In the meantime, be wise, wary, and watchful, lest all this end in tragedy yet again.

Please tell Yorick I said he is to behave, and that the answer to his riddle is "Seven chickens."

Sincerely,
S. H. Elives

"Drat!" said the skull, after Charlie had read the letter out loud. "I thought for sure I had him stumped that time."

"Forget the chickens," said Charlie crossly. "What about all this danger stuff?"

"I told you I was nervous. You wouldn't believe me."

"I don't understand. No offense, but what could hurt you? I mean, you're already..." Charlie let his voice trail off.

"Ever hear the phrase *a fate worse than death*? Anyway, the old man didn't say *I* was in danger. He said *you* were entering a time of great danger."

Charlie felt his throat go dry. "Are you serious?"

"I'm a jester! Why should I be serious? However, I *am* telling the truth, if that's what you want to know."

"What can we do about it?"

"Nothing, yet. So why don't you worry about the immediate problems instead? For instance, what are you going to do in school tomorrow?"

"I don't have the slightest idea," groaned Charlie. He shrugged. "Probably I should just go in with a big paper bag over my head."

"Oh, you're not *that* ugly. And I wish you wouldn't do that."

"Do what?"

"Shrug like that."

"Why not?" asked Charlie, baffled at the suggestion.

"Because I can't."

"So?" he asked, shrugging again without even realizing it.

Yorick sighed. "Well, sometimes the best way to answer a question is with a shrug, the way you just did. Only, since I don't have any shoulders, I can't do it! So it's very annoying to have to watch you do it. I mean, it's like you're rubbing it in. Do you suppose you could get rid of your shoulders for a while? Oh, forget it. I suppose that's not possible. On the other hand (which I don't have, either, now that I think of it) you could—"

"Shut up, will you!" snapped Charlie. He got up and stalked out of the room, then out of the house. Though he had told himself he was leaving because he couldn't stand any more of the skull's chatter, as he walked he realized that what he was most upset about wasn't the skull, or Karen Ackerman. It was Gilbert. Until Charlie found a way to make things right with him, the knot in his stomach wasn't going to go away.

Without actually intending to, Charlie found himself circling his house, then cutting through the cemetery toward Gilbert's place, which also bordered on the graveyard. Not wanting to come out in Gilbert's backyard, he ducked through Old Man Grimsby's orchard, then out onto the sidewalk.

Cautiously, he walked toward the Dawkins's house.

Gilbert was sitting on his front porch, reading. When Charlie saw this he turned and headed back toward the corner. He walked to the next corner. Then he turned and walked back far enough that he could see Gilbert's porch again.

Gilbert was still there, looking pale and frail and very bald as he turned the pages of a large book.

Charlie took a deep breath and started forward. After three steps he turned back. If he was going to talk to Gilbert, and if he wanted to avoid another catastrophe, he had better practice the conversation first. After all, he couldn't offer any little white lies ("Gee, you sure look great without any hair!") in order to make Gilbert feel better. Whatever he said was going to have to be the absolute truth.

Ducking behind a wide hickory tree where he would be out of sight should Gilbert look up, Charlie leaned against the rough bark and thought about what he could say to his friend that was true.

Well, to begin with, he really *was* sorry for what he had said on Friday. And he really hadn't meant to hurt Gilbert's feelings. And he really did want to apologize for—

No, better watch out. That last one wasn't quite true. He hated apologizing. But he did want to set things right with Gilbert, if only so this nasty feeling in his stomach would go away.

Charlie sighed. That sounded so selfish!

He tried it again, changing the last part: "I really do want to set things right with Gilbert. I'm worried about him."

Hmmm. That must be true, too. And it certainly sounded better. Of course, worrying about sounding better—

He squashed the thought, realizing he was starting a circle of ideas that could ripple on forever.

What else could he say to Gilbert? Not much, he decided, since most of the things that were true were not very nice—and most of the things that were nice weren't true. For example, even though Mr. Diogen had assured the class that Gilbert's illness was not contagious and there was no way any of them could catch it, Charlie continued to feel a twist of fear at the very sight of Gilbert. And some deep, treacherous part of his mind still suspected it might be dangerous even to talk to him.

He didn't really believe that—and yet at the same time he *did* believe it. Charlie sighed. Where was the truth in that kind of situation?

He reviewed the few respectable truths he had managed to come up with, then gathered his courage and started toward Gilbert's house for the fourth time. He was terrified—more frightened, he realized, than when Mark and his gang had chased him into the swamp. Even so, it would be better to take care of this now than at school tomorrow.

Another nasty truth, thought Charlie regretfully. He would have liked to believe he was being entirely noble by going to see Gilbert. The truth, of course, was that he was trying to smooth things over today so he wouldn't have to deal with them in front of the entire class tomorrow.

Cripe, he couldn't even lie to *himself* anymore!

Moving quietly, he walked up to Gilbert's front porch. Gilbert didn't look up from his book. Charlie wondered if Gilbert didn't hear him or was just pretending not to notice him. He thought about making a noise to attract Gilbert's attention, but he was so nervous about what he was going to say when Gilbert finally did look up that he couldn't bring himself to do it.

He stood in silence at the base of the steps, studying Gilbert. He remembered times they had sat on that porch together, reading comic books and drinking lemonade that Gilbert's mom had made fresh. He and Gilbert had been pretty close friends in the third and fourth grades. But in the last year or so they had drifted apart. Not for any particular reason, no fight or anything; they just hadn't seen as much of each other.

Or was there a reason? Charlie wondered suddenly. Had Gilbert's illness been starting back then? Was that why he had stopped coming out to play so often, not spent as much time with the other kids?

Charlie felt his stomach add another knot to the mess already there. If he had been paying more attention, he might have figured out something was wrong. He might have been a better friend than he had been.

Gilbert still didn't notice him.

Finally Charlie whistled three high notes, then one long, low one. Their old signal.

Gilbert put down his book and looked up.

NINE

Gilbert

"Hi," said Gilbert. That was all. Just "Hi."

Charlie realized he had secretly been hoping Gilbert would make this easy for him, would say, "Don't worry, Charlie. I understand. I'm not mad."

But he just sat there, holding his book.

"So, how you doing?" asked Charlie.

Gilbert shrugged. "Not real great."

Suddenly Charlie's worries about himself faded into the background as he realized yet one more truth: Though he had been assuming that sooner or later Gilbert was going to get better, he had no idea if that was really the case. Maybe Gilbert *wasn't* going to get better.

Ever.

Charlie felt his knees wobble. Forcing his legs to stay under control, he climbed the steps. "I'm sorry," he said when he got to the top. "About Friday. About what I said. It was stupid. I didn't mean to, it just came out. After I said it I wished—"

He broke off. He had been about to say he had wished he was dead, but that wasn't true. He swallowed, then finished lamely, "I wished I hadn't."

"I wished you hadn't, too," said Gilbert, with a small laugh.

Charlie nodded. Looking at the spot that used to be his, where he had spent so many hours reading and talking and laughing, he said, "Can I sit down?" Then, before Gilbert could answer, his traitor mouth opened again and asked, "Is it safe?"

Gilbert closed his eyes. "It's safe, Charlie. You can't catch what I have."

"How did you get it?" asked Charlie, settling nervously into his old spot.

Gilbert shrugged. "No one knows for sure. It's just something that goes wrong in your body. But it's not catching. And it has a name, Charlie. I have—had—cancer. They cut it out. But I have to have treatment to make sure it doesn't come back. That's what made my hair fall out. It makes me puke a lot, too. And feel tired. I hate it. I hate it more than I can tell you."

Charlie felt tears start up in his eyes.

Before he could say anything Gilbert's face hardened, and he turned away. The pale skin of his head gleamed in the afternoon sun, making it look almost like—a skull.

"I'm sorry," said Charlie, reaching out to touch his shoulder.

Gilbert turned back, and it was as if a curtain had been drawn behind his eyes. "I didn't mean to say all that," he muttered.

Charlie wondered if the curse of the skull was stretching out from him, forcing Gilbert to speak the truth as well. Aloud he said, "Can I help?"

Gilbert shrugged again. "Not unless you want to take my treatments for me. But I don't think that would do either of us any good."

Charlie laughed. But it was just a small laugh. An uncomfortable one. Because, watching Gilbert shrug, he had just figured out what he had to do to make things up to him.

And he didn't like it.

Not one bit.

"Gilbert," called a voice from inside the house, "I want you to come in and take your nap now."

Gilbert sighed. "That sounds so baby!"

But Charlie, hearing the tiredness in his friend's voice, knew it was time to leave. "Well, I'll see you later," he said.

"Yeah," said Gilbert. "See you later."

All the way home Charlie fought the idea that had hit him on the porch. He really didn't want to do it. But something inside him kept whispering that it was the only way to redeem himself, the only way to make things up with Gilbert.

And below that, an even softer voice insisted it was the *right* thing for him to do.

He was so wrapped up in trying to figure it all out that he forgot to stop and get a gift for Gramma Ethel's birthday—which meant that when he got home he had to rush up to his room and make her a card.

"What are you doing?" asked Yorick, when Charlie pulled out a piece of paper and some old crayons.

"Making a card for my great-grandmother."

"Ah. Forgot to buy her a gift, huh?"

Charlie tried to deny it, but the words wouldn't come out of his mouth. So instead he said, rather sharply, "Why ask a question if you already know the answer?"

"To be annoying," replied Yorick happily.

Charlie had no doubt that this was true.

He was still working on the card, which was coming out better than he expected, when the first of the guests arrived and his mother called him downstairs. He took the back steps, which led directly into the kitchen.

"Aunt Hilda and Uncle Horace are here," said his mother, who was mashing a big pot of potatoes.

"I know," said Charlie with a grin. "I can see Aunt Hilda's calling card."

He pointed to a bowl of green-Jell-O-and-cottage-cheese salad sitting on the counter. Aunt Hilda had brought it to every family dinner she'd come to for as long as Charlie could remember.

"Well, I've still got a lot to do in here," said Mrs. Eggleston, giving the potatoes another whump. "So I want you to go into the living room and entertain them."

Charlie groaned. Aunt Hilda and Uncle Horace—who were actually his great-aunt and -uncle—were very nice people. Unfortunately, they were also lead-ing contenders for the title "The Two Most Boring People on the Planet."

When he said so, his mother replied, "Well they bore me, too, Charlie. But I want you to go talk to them anyway."

Then she blinked, looking surprised, and somewhat nervous.

Feeling even more nervous than his mother looked, Charlie went into the living room, where his aunt and uncle waited.

"Hey-hey-hey!" cried Uncle Horace as Charlie entered the room. "It's the Chuckster! How you doing, boy? Take any wooden nickels lately?"

"Now, Horace!" said Aunt Hilda sharply. Then she turned to Charlie, spread her arms, and said, "Come here, my little Charlie-boy, and give me a kiss."

Abandoning his desperate hope that his aunt and uncle might have been kidnapped by aliens and given personality transplants since he last saw them, Charlie went to receive his aunt's enthusiastic kiss (including the ritual wiping away of her lipstick with a crumpled Kleenex from her purse) and his uncle's vigorous handshake. Then he sat a safe distance away and tried to answer their questions about school, life, and the family without saying anything too embarrassing. He wondered where his sisters were. His father, he was pretty sure, was hiding.

"So how are things at school?" asked Aunt Hilda.

"Pretty awful," said Charlie, before he could stop himself.

"Oh, I'm sorry to hear that," said Aunt Hilda sincerely. "What's happened, sweetheart?"

It wasn't an unreasonable question. For the past three years Charlie had cheerfully been telling Aunt Hilda things at school were great, no matter how good or bad they actually were. So naturally she would be interested in this change.

He sighed. "Well, to begin with, my entire class hates me."

Aunt Hilda's eyes widened in alarm. "Why would you ever think such a thing?"

Before he could answer, the doorbell rang. "I'll get it!" he shouted, leaping to his feet in relief.

It was Uncle Bennie and Gramma Ethel. Standing behind them was Bennie's storytelling teacher. She had on a silk blouse whose colors kept shifting, and long, dangling earrings. She looked at Charlie with a clear, direct gaze that somehow made him feel both comfortable and nervous at the same time.

"Hey, Charlie," said Uncle Bennie, reaching forward to tousle his hair. "How you doing?" Fortunately he did not seem to expect an actual answer to this, since he immediately added, "You remember Hyacinth Priest, don't you?"

"Of course," said Charlie, relieved to have a question that was so easy to answer truthfully. Looking up at her, he added, "I liked your stories." He stepped back from the door. "Come on in. Aunt Hilda and Uncle Horace are here already."

"I hope your mother has the coffeepot going," muttered Gramma Ethel. "It's the only way I'll stay awake if I have to sit and listen to those two old bores."

Hyacinth Priest raised an eyebrow but said nothing. Charlie, uncertain whether the comment was a side effect of the curse, or just Gramma Ethel being Gramma Ethel, led the way into the living room. Once there, Uncle Bennie introduced Hyacinth Priest to Uncle Horace and Aunt Hilda.

Charlie's father showed up a minute later, with Mimi and Tiffany at his side. "We went out for a walk," he explained to the gathering. "Didn't want to get caught alone with Uncle Horace and Aunt Hilda."

He blinked and looked startled, then laughed as if he had intended the comment as a joke. The others laughed, too, all except Charlie. But it was an uneasy kind of laugh, and Aunt Hilda looked sad.

"Excuse me a second," said Charlie. Once out of the room, he shot up the stairs. Throwing open the closet door, he pulled Yorick from the shelf and stared directly into his empty eye sockets. "Do you know what's going on down there?" he demanded.

"Bingo?" asked Yorick, his eye sockets glowing into life.

"Truth-or-consequences would be more like it! Come on, I've got to get you out of here."

"Unwanted! Unloved! Homeless again!" Yorick moaned. "Mr. Elives isn't going to like this, kid."

"It's just for the time being," said Charlie urgently. "So we can get through this meal without killing each other."

Yorick sighed. "Ah, the joy of family. Well, I'm used to it. I've spent most of my life—most of my death, for that matter—feeling about as welcome as

105

a beetle in the lemonade. Go ahead. Haul me out, you coldhearted brute."

Charlie pushed down the twinge of guilt he felt, and found a box big enough to hold Yorick. "You'd better not leave me in here overnight!" said the skull, as Charlie closed the flaps.

"I won't. I promise."

He started down the back steps with the box. Unfortunately his mother was still in the kitchen. "Oh, good!" she said. "You did get something for Gramma Ethel. Thank you for remembering, sweetheart."

"This isn't for Gramma!" said Charlie desperately. "It's just something I have to take out to the garage."

"Oh," she said, sounding disappointed. "Well, you can do that later. Right now I need you to finish setting the table."

"But, Mom, I have to—"

"Later, Charlie. Put that in the broom closet for now."

"But—"

"Charlie, please. No excuses."

She wiped a strand of hair off her damp forehead, and Charlie suddenly noticed how tired she looked. Even so, he couldn't leave the skull inside.

"Just let me—"

"*Now,* Charlie!" she said, in a tone that left no room for negotiating. "Put the box in the closet, wash your hands, and set the table."

Charlie felt his stomach sink. Instead of getting

the skull away from the action, all he had managed to do was get it closer to the site of the family dinner.

"This isn't going to be pretty," he muttered as he placed the box in the broom closet.

"It rarely is," said Yorick.

Things didn't go too badly for the first five minutes. Aunt Hilda and Uncle Horace were boring, but that was nothing new. Gramma Ethel was grumpy and cantankerous, but that was nothing new, either. Mr. Eggleston was quieter than usual, possibly as a result of his earlier outburst of unvarnished truth. Uncle Bennie teased Mimi and Tiffany, which they loved. Mrs. Eggleston bustled back and forth from the kitchen with heaping bowls of food. And Hyacinth Priest watched everything with a quiet smile that seemed to indicate she liked what she saw.

The trouble began with Aunt Hilda's green-Jell-O-and-cottage-cheese salad. "Uck," said Mimi, when Mr. Eggleston put a square of it onto her plate. "I *hate* that stuff!"

"Mimi!" said Mrs. Eggleston sharply.

"Oh, let the girl be," said Gramma Ethel. "I hate the stuff, too. Looks like mold, for heaven's sake."

Aunt Hilda gasped, and her face wrinkled into a pucker of dismay.

"I kind of like it," said Uncle Bennie cheerfully.

"You can have mine if you want," said Uncle Horace, lifting his plate hopefully. "To tell you the truth, I never cared much for it myself."

"*Horace!*" cried Aunt Hilda.

Uncle Horace blinked, then glared around the table, as if trying to figure out who had actually said the words that just came out of his mouth.

"I'd like some, please," said Hyacinth Priest gravely.

Aunt Hilda smiled and passed her the salad.

"So, Bennie," said Mr. Eggleston, in a desperate attempt to get the conversation moving again. "How's the storytelling going? Learn to do 'Little Red Riding Hood' yet?"

"Bennie is struggling with stories that have more personal meaning to him," said Ms. Priest quietly.

"If Bennie had any ambition he'd stop fooling around with nonsense like that and learn to do something that would pay him more money," said Aunt Hilda.

Everyone looked at her in surprise.

Ms. Priest smiled. "Perhaps. Do you know the story of the three boys whose mother named them with her wishes for them?"

Aunt Hilda, who was blushing slightly, shook her head.

"Then I shall share it with you," said Ms. Priest. "A brief version only, for it is a story that can take a lifetime to learn, and another lifetime to tell." She took a moment to look at each person sitting at the table.

Then she began.

TEN

The Truth Will Out

"Once, very long ago, there lived a woman who had three sons in three years. When the first boy was born she named him Do-As-You-Should. When the second arrived she named him Do-As-You're-Told. And when the third came to her she named him Do-As-You-Love. This happened in a time when the world knew better the power of names, and so these names had great strength."

Charlie stared as Ms. Priest in astonishment, wondering how she could tell such a story with the skull nearby.

"Now, Do-As-You-Should was a very good boy, and everyone marveled at how well behaved he was. He worked hard and never let his mother down. When he left home he married a good woman, and they had three children of their own.

"Do-As-You're-Told was not quite as good a boy. Oh, it was not that he did anything wrong. He just didn't do much of anything at all, unless he was directed to it. When he left home he married a strong woman, and she kept him on track—though I must say that it was a full-time job, and he tired her out.

"Do-As-You-Love was far and away the worst of the three boys, at least as far as the villagers were concerned. They felt he did not work as hard as his brothers, and that he rarely did anything useful. When Do-As-You-Love left home, it took much longer for him to find a wife, for he was not seen as having good prospects. The woman he finally did marry was much pitied by her friends. Oddly enough, they had a very happy marriage.

"Now, as the years went by, a strange thing happened. While Do-As-You-Should grew to a position of prominence in his village and Do-As-You're-Told came to be seen as a proper citizen, it was Do-As-You-Love that people thought of most often, sought out, asked advice of. The only advice he ever gave, though, was to repeat his own name: 'Do as you love,' he would tell people. 'Then you will be happy.'

"Usually they would explain why this was not possible, and go away feeling cheated and let down.

"Eventually Do-As-You-Should died, which should be no surprise to anyone. He went straight to heaven, which is probably no surprise, either. Once there he was taken before the Almighty, who granted him one wish.

" 'I want nothing but a chance to rest,' said Do-As-You-Should, 'for I have worked hard, and I am tired.'

"And his wish was granted.

"The next year Do-As-You're-Told died. Alas, when *he* reached the gates of heaven, he was not taken to see the Almighty, nor granted a wish of any kind. Instead, he was sent back to try again, because doing only what you're told is not nearly enough."

Ms. Priest picked up a piece of bread and began to butter it.

"But what about Do-As-You-Love?" demanded Tiffany. "Did he die, too?"

Ms. Priest smiled. "Oh, of course he did. We all do, eventually."

"Well, what happened when *he* went to heaven?"

Ms. Priest shrugged. "He never noticed the difference."

Mr. Eggleston snorted. "That's the stupidest story I ever heard."

Ms. Priest raised an elegant eyebrow and said softly, "Perhaps you did not listen properly."

"Oh, he listened," said Gramma Ethel. "He just didn't want to hear. Cut a little too close to the bone, didn't it, butcher boy?"

"Gramma!" gasped Mrs. Eggleston.

"I suppose you've always done what you loved, Ethel?" asked Mr. Eggleston sharply.

"It's not that simple, Archie," said Gramma Ethel, spearing a brussels sprout with her fork. "Sometimes one want runs into another. I wanted to be a mother. Once you do that, you stop doing a lot of other things you love, at least for a while."

"What did you do before you were a mother?" asked Charlie.

A wrinkled smile crossed Gramma Ethel's face. "I was an ecdysiast. I was darn good at it, too."

"What's an eckdizzy?" asked Tiffany.

Gramma Ethel's smile broadened. Stretching out her hands she gave her chest a shake and said, "An ecdysiast is a striptease dancer."

Uncle Horace spit coffee across the table and Aunt Hilda choked on a mouthful of green-Jell-O-and-cottage-cheese salad. Uncle Bennie hooted with laughter.

"Gramma," said Mrs. Eggleston sharply. "Not in front of the children!"

"Oh, bosh, Veronica! It's not going to hurt the little dears. What's worse—the truth, or all the lies we tell to protect them, all the secrets we keep pushing under the rug?"

"I don't think there's a lot of that going on around here, Ethel," said Mr. Eggleston. His voice was sharp, but Charlie noticed a nervous edge in it as well. He wondered if his father had some secret he was afraid might be revealed.

"Of course there's not," said Mrs. Eggleston firmly. But she looked nervous, too.

Gramma Ethel fairly cackled at their response. "No secrets, eh? Let's see. Did you ever tell the kids about your first marriage, Veronica?"

"You were married before?" cried Charlie in astonishment.

Mimi turned to Mr. Eggleston. "Are you my real father?" she asked nervously.

"Of course I'm your real father!" His voice was

firm and gentle at the same time, but Charlie could sense the anger underneath it. Raising his head to look toward the other end of the table, Mr. Eggleston said sharply, "Ethel, that's enough!"

Gramma Ethel shrugged and put a forkful of mashed potatoes in her mouth.

"We'll talk about this later, children," said Mrs. Eggleston. Turning to Ms. Priest, she added, "I'm sorry you had to hear all that. It's not usually like that here."

"That's true," said Uncle Horace. "Generally it's a lot more boring."

"Look who's talking about boring!" snapped Mrs. Eggleston. Then she blinked and said, "Excuse me, I have to go check on the dessert."

"Do you think I like being boring, Veronica?" asked Uncle Horace mournfully, as Mrs. Eggleston pushed herself away from the table. "I hate it!"

It had never occurred to Charlie that Uncle Horace might actually *know* he was boring. Suddenly Charlie felt an odd kind of sympathy for him. Maybe for Uncle Horace being boring was like lying had been for Charlie before he got the skull: He knew he was doing it, but he couldn't stop himself.

Mrs. Eggleston paused at the kitchen door. "I'm sorry," she said. Then she hurried into the kitchen, leaving them to wonder if she was apologizing to Uncle Horace or to the table at large.

"Perhaps I should go," said Ms. Priest quietly.

"Please don't," said Uncle Bennie. He sounded almost desperate.

"Oh-ho! Is she your girlfriend, Bennie?" asked Aunt Hilda. "At last, a girlfriend! I'm so pleased. But don't you think she's a little old for you?"

Bennie rolled his eyes. "What has gotten into everyone around here?" he asked in exasperation.

"Truth attack," said Charlie, before he could stop himself.

Bennie took a deep breath, then said, "Well, Aunt Hilda, the truth is I'm *never* going to have a girlfriend. I have a boyfriend. His name is Dave. And if this family would recognize that, it would make my life a lot easier!"

Aunt Hilda gasped and burst into tears. Uncle Horace turned red. Gramma Ethel smacked her spoon on her plate and shouted, "Hot damn! It's about time you spoke up, boy! I was getting awfully tired of watching you hide the truth."

"You knew?" asked Bennie in astonishment.

Gramma Ethel scowled at him. "Just how stupid do you think I am?"

"Actually, I think you're quite a smart old dame. I just wish you weren't so cranky."

"So do I. On the other hand, when you're as old as I am, speaking your mind is one of the few pleasures you have left."

Uncle Bennie turned to Charlie's father. "What about you, Archie?"

Mr. Eggleston shrugged. "Your sister and I figured it out a few years ago."

Bennie looked troubled. "Why didn't you say something?"

"Why didn't *you?*"

Bennie started to answer, stopped, then started again. "I was ... I thought you ... I wanted ..." He closed his eyes, as if thinking very hard, then sighed. "I was afraid."

"You should have given us more credit, Bennie," said Mrs. Eggleston softly. She was standing just inside the door from the kitchen, holding the coffeepot. "I'm not going to stop loving my baby brother just because of something like that."

Charlie, who had been staring at his uncle through all this, couldn't believe what he had heard. His stomach was churning, and he could feel tears pricking at the corners of his eyes. Suddenly he couldn't stand to stay at the table anymore. Jumping to his feet, he bolted from the room.

"Charlie!" cried Uncle Bennie, reaching for him. "Wait!"

"Let him go, Bennie," said Mr. Eggleston softly. "I'll talk to him later."

That was the last Charlie heard. Snatching the box that held the skull from the broom closet, he raced out of the house. In the backyard, he glanced around for a moment, then headed for the cemetery. Pushing his way through the hedge that separated it from their lawn, he stumbled forward among the moonlit tombstones. About a hundred feet in he tripped over a low stone and almost fell. Stopping to catch his breath, he resisted a momentary urge to fling the skull against one of the stones and shatter it into a thousand pieces.

He walked on, more slowly now. Ahead was a clump of oak trees where he sometimes went to think when he was upset.

He trudged toward the oaks and took a seat on one of the fallen tombstones that lay beneath them. After a moment he removed the skull from the box and placed it on another of the stones, so that it was face-to-face with him. He stared at it for a long time. Finally, in a low, fierce voice, he whispered, "How do I get rid of you?"

Yorick's eyes began to glow, a sight that was more eerie than usual in the darkness beneath the trees. "Whoa!" said the skull. "Why so hostile? Bad day at the OK Corral?"

"You're ruining my life!" cried Charlie.

"Hey, let's not confuse a temporary problem with a ruined life."

"The skull has a point," said a soft voice nearby.

Charlie jumped up. "Ms. Priest! What are *you* doing here?"

"I thought you could use someone to talk to," said the librarian. She was standing in a small puddle of moonlight, just outside the cluster of oaks. "Someone besides Yorick, that is," she added, gesturing toward the skull.

Charlie's eyes widened. "You know Yorick?"

"Alas, I know him well."

"We're old friends," said the skull cheerfully. "Hi-ho, Hyacinth. How ya doin'?"

"A little tired," said Ms. Priest, "but other than that quite well. Much better than poor Charlie here."

"But how do you know each other?" persisted Charlie.

"I occasionally work with Mr. Elives," said Ms. Priest.

"I never have been able to figure out the exact arrangement," said the skull.

"Perhaps that's because you have no need to," the storyteller replied smoothly. "Anyway, what's important right now is helping Charlie get things settled. That, and figuring out just who—or what— is after *you*, Yorick. But first things first." She gestured to a nearby tombstone. "May I?"

It took Charlie a moment to realize she was asking if she could sit down. "Go ahead," he said, without any enthusiasm.

She turned and blew at the top of the stone. Though she made just the tiniest of puffs, the dirt and leaves vanished completely. She brushed the top of the stone with the tip of her index finger, nodded in satisfaction, then gathered her colorful skirt and sat.

"Difficult evening, wasn't it?" she said casually.

"You're not kidding," said Charlie. "And you weren't even around for the part with Gilbert."

"Who's Gilbert?"

"My friend. I hurt his feelings, and now I have to do something about it. I mean, I did do something, in a way, because I went and talked to him. But I need to do something more."

"Have you decided what?"

"I think so. But I don't want to talk about it."

Ms. Priest smiled. "A truthful answer. Evasive, but truthful."

"We could have used more of that evasive stuff at dinner. Which reminds me—how come you could tell that story at the table? Since you know about Yorick, you must know that you have to tell the truth while you're around him."

"But I did tell the truth."

Charlie narrowed his eyes. "Are you trying to tell me that story really happened?"

Hyacinth Priest laughed, a merry sound that seemed to press back the edges of the night. "Of course not. But there are many kinds of truth, Charlie, and that story is true in a very deep way."

"This truth stuff is more complicated than I thought," muttered Charlie.

"I suspect that's true of most things," said Ms. Priest.

"I think I liked it better when I didn't know that," said Charlie. "In fact, there's a lot of things I'd rather I didn't know."

"You mean like about Bennie?" she asked softly.

"Definitely."

She smiled sadly. "For my part, I'm glad Bennie said what he did. I think it will make his life easier."

Charlie shrugged morosely.

"Does it change things for you that much?"

Charlie thought for a minute. He started to say, "Well, I can't go places with Dave and Bennie anymore," but the words, not being true, wouldn't come out of his mouth. He frowned and tried again.

"I won't feel good going places with Dave and Bennie anymore."

"Why not?"

"Well, what will people think?" he asked, as if he was talking to a moron.

Ms. Priest raised an eyebrow. "What did people think that last time you went someplace with Bennie and Dave?"

"I don't know!" he said savagely. Then, seized by the need to speak the absolute truth, he added, "Nothing, probably. But this is different."

Well, that must be true. If only she wouldn't ask—

"Why?"

Charlie sighed. "Because *I* feel different."

Ms. Priest nodded, seeming content to leave it there.

"Don't you want to know why?" asked Charlie suspiciously.

"I think I can figure it out."

"And she's going to let *you* figure out whether your reasons are any good or not," added the skull.

"Perhaps, Yorick, you should tend to your own business," Ms. Priest said softly.

"I'm not a businessman," sniffed the skull. "I am an artiste."

"And where is it written that you can't be both? Anyway, businessman or artiste, you still have to deal with whatever is heading your way."

"Do you have any idea what it is?" asked Yorick, suddenly serious.

Ms. Priest shook her head. "I do not. Nor does the old man. All we know is that it is both strange and powerful."

Without intending to, Charlie made a small gasp.

"We don't think it's after you, Charlie," said Ms. Priest calmly. "Even so, I urge you to be wise, wary, and watchful. I have to go now. You can find me at the library if you need me."

"Wait!" said Charlie and Yorick together. But she shook her head and, without saying another word, stepped swiftly and silently out of the grove of trees.

The Great
Toad Fiasco

Charlie watched her walk away, then shivered as he saw her step into a patch of mist from which she did not reappear.

"Women," said the skull.

Charlie wasn't sure what Yorick meant, but he figured it must be true. He thought for a second, then said, "Well, now what?"

"Go back inside?" suggested Yorick.

He shook his head. "Not yet."

"All right, then why don't you tell me a story. To be more specific, why don't you tell me the story about why *you* always tell stories. I figure there must be a reason."

"I don't like to talk about it."

"Hey, I don't like talking about some of the things that happened to me, but I showed them to you anyway. That's what friends do. It's part of how you get to know each other."

"Who said I want to be friends?"

"Boy, no wonder you're in trouble in school. If I had feet, I'd be outta here myself."

Charlie sighed. He had known it was a rotten thing to say even as the words were passing his lips. "Sorry." Then, because he still felt guilty, he added, "Okay, I'll tell you."

He took a deep breath.

"My mother still calls it The Great Toad Fiasco. It happened back in second grade. Me and Gilbert and Mark Evans were pretty good friends that year." Charlie paused. It had been so long since he'd thought about what happened back then that he had almost forgotten he used to be friends with Mark. "We hung out on the playground together, stayed over at each other's houses. Stuff like that."

"Sounds nice," said Yorick, and for a moment Charlie almost got the impression he was jealous.

"So anyway, one day Gilbert found this big old toad on the playground. I mean really big, the kind that fills both your hands."

Charlie's mind drifted back as he started to tell the story, so that he almost felt as if he were on the playground again, with the hot sun beating down on him, the shouts and shrieks going on all around, the toad heavy and dry in his hands.

"While I was holding it, I suddenly remembered something. 'My uncle Bennie told me if you put a toad's head in your mouth and count to a hundred, you'll be able to talk toad talk,' I told the guys.

"Gilbert said I was full of baloney. But Mark said,

'No, Gil, it's true. Toads are about the most magical animals there are.'

" 'Fine,' said Gilbert. 'Then *you* put his head in your mouth.'

"Mark shook his head. 'It has to be the one who found him. That's part of the magic.'

" 'I didn't know that,' I said."

Charlie shook his own head at the memory. "I was so dumb back then! I thought it was cool that Mark knew about the toad-talk thing, since I had never heard it from anyone but Uncle Bennie before. I didn't have enough brains to see he was just trying to get Gilbert to do it."

"I know the type," said Yorick.

"Anyway, Gilbert took the toad back and looked at him as if he was really thinking about doing it.

" 'I hear they know amazing secrets,' Mark whispered.

"Before I knew it, Gilbert opened his mouth and stuck the toad in headfirst as far as it would go."

Yorick laughed. "Whatta yutz!"

"Hey, we were only in second grade. Second graders will believe anything. Anyway, that was when the teacher showed up. She saw the toad's butt sticking out of Gilbert's mouth and shouted, 'Gilbert Dawkins, you spit that out right this minute!'

"Gilbert did. The toad came flying out. I caught it. I didn't mean to, it was one of those reflex things. Its head was all covered with spit, and it felt disgusting, so I tossed it away."

"You tossed it away?"

"Well, actually, I threw it to the teacher." Charlie

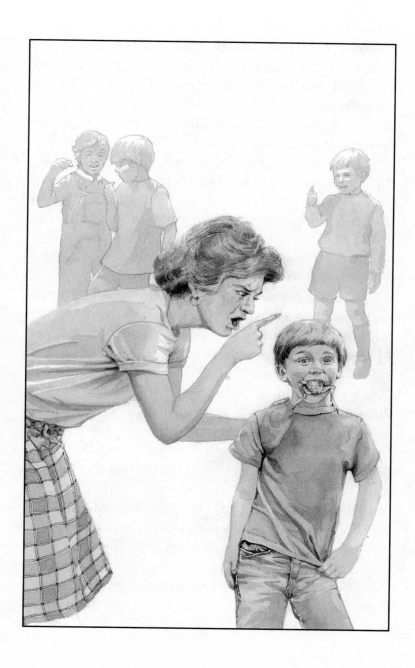

shuddered at the memory. "She was not amused. At least the toad was okay, except for being scared. And offended, maybe. When she put it down, it looked pretty cranky."

Yorick snickered. "Wouldn't you, under those circumstances?"

"I suppose. Anyway, if the toad was cranky, Mrs. Pitwing was even crankier. 'Just *what* is going on here?' she asked. Gilbert started to blubber. 'Charlie told me if I put the toad in my mouth I would be able to talk toad talk!'

"Mrs. Pitwing turned to me. 'Charlie, is that true?'

"I didn't know if she was asking me if I really said it, or if it was really true about learning to talk toad talk. Remember, I was only in second grade. So I just nodded my head. 'Mark said it, too,' I added.

" 'I did not!' said Mark.

"I couldn't believe he was lying like that! 'You did too!'

" 'Did not!'

" '*Liar!*' I shouted.

"The teacher turned to Gilbert. 'Did Mark say it, too?'

"Gilbert looked at me. He looked at Mark. Then he shook his head. 'Just Charlie,' he whispered."

"Ouch!" said Yorick. "What a letdown. So what happened next?"

"What do you think happened? I got in trouble. I got in trouble with the teacher. I got in trouble with my parents. I got in trouble with Gilbert's parents. I even got in trouble with Mark's parents, because they claimed I was trying to blame their precious baby for what I had done. Anyway, that was when I gave up on the truth. Bennie had lied to me, though he was just fooling around. Mark had lied about me. Even Gilbert lied. I was the only one who told the truth that day, and I was the only one who got in trouble."

"How come Gilbert lied, anyway?" asked Yorick.

"I asked him about that a couple of weeks later, when I was finally talking to him again. He said Mark would have beat him up if he hadn't. Which was probably true. Anyway, after that I noticed that Mrs. Pitwing never believed me, no matter what I said. So I figured, why bother, and started telling her lies. I started with little ones, things about what had happened to my homework, stuff like that. Then I started inventing things to make myself seem more important at school. Pretty soon I was inventing stories to get sympathy at home. After a while I got so used to lying that I didn't even think about it. And you want to know something weird? At first almost everyone (except Mrs. Pitwing) believed me, because they were used to me telling the truth. Then they started to figure it out. These days *no one* believes me, even when I do tell the truth! So what's truth got to do with anything, anyway?"

"Don't ask me," said Yorick bitterly.

"Anyway, I stopped being friends with Mark after that. I almost stopped being friends with Gilbert, but he was really sorry for lying about me, plus he pointed out that if I hadn't told that stupid toad story to begin with, none of it would have happened. So I forgave him."

Charlie sighed. "We used to be really good friends. I wish I hadn't hurt his feelings on Friday." Suddenly he stood up. "I have to go do something."

"Hey!" shouted the skull. "Don't leave me here."

Charlie hesitated for a moment. Then he picked up the skull, put it in the box, and walked back through the cemetery to his house.

The company had left. From the sound of things, his parents were in the living room. Charlie slipped up the back stairs and returned the skull to his closet. Then he sat on the edge of his bed, trying to gather his courage for what he needed to do next.

Yorick remained mercifully quiet.

Though he knew what he wanted to do, Charlie's mind kept racing in different directions. There was so much to think about: Gilbert, his grandmother, his mother's previous marriage, Uncle Bennie's revelation.

He wondered how many more secrets his family had. Did every family have secrets like this, kept hidden and covered up, festering in the darkness? And was it better to keep them hidden—or to bring them out into the light?

Well, for better or worse, a batch of the Eggleston secrets had been unearthed.

Now the family had to live with them.

Of course, the ones who'd had the secrets had been living with them all along. Charlie wondered what it had been like for Uncle Bennie to live hiding the fact that he loved someone, cared about someone, hiding it because he feared the family would scorn him if they found out.

And how did he feel now that his secret had come to light?

Curiosity and concern outweighing his nervousness, Charlie decided to go ask his parents about Bennie.

And after that—well, he might talk to them about the other thing, too, the thing he needed to do to make things right with Gilbert.

Or maybe not.

He tiptoed as he went down the stairs, just in case he decided to change his mind at the last minute.

The tiptoeing didn't do him any good. His parents heard him coming, something he could tell by the way their voices dropped to whispers.

He paused on the steps.

"Charlie?" called his mother, after a moment.

"Yeah?"

"Come on down and talk to us."

Relieved, in a way, that the decision was made for him, he clumped down the stairs and into the living room.

"How are you?" asked his father gently.

He shrugged. He had expected them to be angry at him. But he suddenly realized that they had no way of knowing that the catastrophic dinner conversation had been all his fault.

"Sorry about Gramma Ethel's birthday," he said softly.

His father laughed. "Don't worry about that, bucko. She said it was the most fun she's had in years."

Charlie smiled. "She would say that. But how about Uncle Bennie? Is he mad at me?"

Mrs. Eggleston shook her head. "Bennie wanted to stay to talk to you, but I told him to let it wait for a while. He did say to tell you good night."

Charlie looked at his mother and found himself trying to imagine her married to someone other than his father. He shook his head to drive away the idea and asked, "Is he all right?"

She smiled. "It's nice of you to ask, Charlie. Bennie is fine. In fact, he was mostly worried about you."

"I'm okay. I just don't like it much, is all. And I don't want anyone to know about it. I've got enough troubles as it is."

Mr. Eggleston spread his hands in front of him. They were thick with muscle from his work at the butcher shop. "Charlie, there's not much you can do about it. Either the information gets around or it doesn't. If it does, you'll probably get some teasing. But not from your true friends."

True friends. How many true friends did he have?

Well, one that he could think of. One that he had hurt very badly.

Looking at his parents, he said, "I need your help."

"To do what?" asked his mother.

"I want to shave my head."

Charlie's mother looked at him in shock for a moment. Then she started to smile. "Why, sweetheart! What a perfectly wonderful idea!"

"It is?" asked Mr. Eggleston in surprise.

"It certainly is," she said, and in her voice Charlie heard a kind of pride in him that he had almost forgotten.

It took a little longer to convince Charlie's father, but once he had heard the whole story and understood what his son was doing, he agreed. "Go for it, Charlie," he said, as he often did. "After all, what's the worst thing that could happen?"

Charlie's mother, on the other hand, despite her approval, asked three times, "Are you *sure* you want to go through with this?"

Three times he answered that he was positive.

That was before they went into the kitchen and actually started the cutting. When Charlie heard the buzz of the clippers he started to panic.

When he felt their cold metal vibrating against the back of his neck he nearly jumped off the stool where he was sitting.

And when he saw the first clump of his straight brown hair hit the floor, it was all he could do to keep from shouting, "Wait! I changed my mind!"

Except he hadn't, really. And even if he had, it would have been too late. He could already feel the wide stripe of bare skin growing on the back of his neck.

Closing his eyes, Charlie tried to keep from trembling.

The buzzing continued.

"All done, champ!" said his father at last.

Charlie slipped from the stool and went to stand in front of the bathroom mirror. Though he knew what to expect, the sight still shocked him. His head suddenly seemed enormous.

What have I done? he thought in horror as he ran his hands over his shiny bare skin.

Then he thought about Gilbert, and realized that at least he, Charlie, had *chosen* to look like this.

Gilbert didn't have a choice.

Well, Karen can't say I didn't try, he told himself—knowing full well that didn't mean she wasn't going to laugh when she saw him.

Suddenly he understood a little of how Gilbert must have felt the night before he returned to school.

His mother came to stand behind him. Putting her hands on his shoulders, she met his eyes in the mirror.

"I think you look very handsome," she whispered.

Charlie figured that must be the truth.

He also figured he couldn't count on most people to see him with the same eyes that his mother did.

"Great bouncing billiard balls!" cried Yorick when Charlie returned to his room. "What happened to you?"

"I shaved off all my hair," said Charlie. "Well, actually my parents shaved it off. But I asked them to."

"Ah. I take it you were so impressed with how incredibly handsome I look sans hair that you decided to try it yourself?"

"Yeah, right. Now be quiet, would you? You've caused enough trouble for one day. I want to think."

It didn't take long for him to give up on that idea. Between the family fiasco, the situation with Uncle Bennie, and his own new state of hairlessness, thinking was an exercise in pain and confusion. Finally he decided to call Gilbert and ask if they could walk to school together the next day.

"I don't walk now, Charlie," said Gilbert, when his mom called him to the phone. "I'm not ready for that yet. But thanks for asking."

"Sure," said Charlie. "No problem." He was too startled to say more; he hadn't realized Gilbert was so fragile.

He was also frustrated. He had wanted to see Gilbert, show him what he had done, *before* they got to school. Somehow just telling him on the phone didn't feel right.

So he kept his mouth shut.

"Holy mackerel!" said Tiffany, when Charlie sat down at the breakfast table the next morning. "What happened to you?"

"Charlie's a baldie!" squealed Mimi.

"Charlie's making a fashion statement," said Mrs. Eggleston. "Leave him alone." Then she winked at Charlie as she set a plate of pancakes in front of him.

When his father offered to drive him to school, Charlie accepted gratefully. He put on a baseball cap and managed to dawdle enough before they left that by the time they got to the building most of the kids were already inside.

"Good luck, champ," said Mr. Eggleston, as Charlie climbed slowly out of the EGGLESTON'S MEAT MARKET van.

"Thanks, Dad. I'll need it."

Torn between feeling triumphantly virtuous and thinking he had finally done the most stupid thing in his entire long history of stupid mistakes, Charlie headed for the building.

TWELVE

The Bald Truth

"Hats off in school," said Mrs. Lincoln automatically, as Charlie came through the door.

Charlie hesitated, then swept off his cap. The principal's eyes widened, but a second later she smiled. "You're in Gilbert Dawkins's class, aren't you? Good work, Charlie."

Feeling a little more solid, he smiled back and headed for the classroom. Even so, he hesitated in the hall before going in. Finally telling himself he was going to have to face the class sooner or later, he counted to three and thrust open the door.

He was greeted by several gasps, a couple of giggles, and a snort of laughter from Mark Evans.

Mr. Diogen, who was standing at his desk, looked startled. But then he winked at Charlie and gave him a thumbs-up sign.

Charlie headed for his seat. As he passed Gilbert, his friend put out his hand.

Charlie held out his own, and they slapped palms.

When the class came back from music, Charlie found a note from Karen Ackerman in his desk: "You did better than I thought you could! You're pretty cool, Charlie."

This reaction was not unanimous. He noticed Mark Evans scowling at him several times throughout the morning, and when the class went outside for recess, Mark and several of his cronies maneuvered Charlie into a corner.

"You think you're pretty smart, don't you, Eggleston?" said Mark.

"Not as smart as I'd like to be," said Charlie truthfully.

"Not as smart as you need to be, you little suck-up," sneered Mark, just before he kicked Charlie in the stomach.

Charlie hit the ground, hard. Mark and his friends turned and headed in different directions, moving casually, as if nothing had happened.

Charlie pulled himself to a sitting position and sat doubled over, clutching his stomach. He was still trying to fight back tears when Gilbert sat down next to him.

"What happened?"

"I don't want to talk about it."

"You never do," said Gilbert.

They sat side by side, their bald heads shining in the sun.

Charlie would have liked to walk home with Gilbert that afternoon but couldn't, of course, because

Gilbert wasn't walking. He also wanted to go back to the swamp. But he was afraid that if he did that, Mark and his gang might jump him again.

So he went straight home. To his pleasure, Karen Ackerman walked part of the way with him.

When he reached his house, he found his uncle sitting on the porch, waiting for him.

"Hey," said Charlie, still standing on the front walk.

"Hey," said Bennie. "Nice haircut."

Charlie blushed.

"Your mom told me about why you did it. I thought it was a terrific idea. How'd it go over at school?"

"Okay," said Charlie, shrugging.

Bennie sighed. "Are you mad at me?"

Charlie thought about that. "No, I'm not mad." Then, remembering the last conversation he'd had with Bennie on this porch, he added, "But I could be. Just last Saturday you sat right here and told me, 'Love is nothing to be ashamed of.' Weren't you embarrassed to be lying like that?"

It was Bennie's turn to blush. "I'll admit I didn't follow my own advice, Charlie. But that doesn't mean I was lying." He looked away for a moment. When he spoke again, his voice was soft. "Sometimes when you say something to someone else, it's because it's what you need to hear yourself. What I said was the truth: I *shouldn't* have been ashamed. I didn't gain anything by hiding the truth, you know. Oh, I probably spared myself a little grief from Aunt Hilda and Uncle Horace. But at the same time I missed out on some real support from your mom and dad." He shrugged. "I didn't want to cause a fuss, I guess.

And I didn't want to lose anyone's respect. But what kind of respect do you have if it's based on a lie, anyway?" He shrugged again. "I'll head out if you want me to. I don't want to make you nervous."

"You don't make me nervous," said Charlie. "Well, maybe a little. Mostly I just think it's yucky."

Bennie laughed. "And I think those bloodthirsty horror stories you read are yucky. Who knows what makes people like what they like? Now listen, I've got a news flash for you."

"I don't know if I can stand another one."

"Well, you're not going to like this one, but you probably ought to know it. There's going to be a town meeting at the library Friday night so Harley Evans can present the plans for that industrial park of his. Dave got a press release on it at the studio this morning. He knows how you feel about the project, so he passed the information on to me."

"What am I supposed to do about it?" asked Charlie, vaguely annoyed that Dave had done something thoughtful.

Bennie shrugged. "Nothing in particular. I just thought you'd want to know."

On Tuesday morning Jeff Parker, Emmett Abbott, and Porky Gibbons came to school with shaved heads. They hung out with Charlie and Gilbert on the playground, and the five of them decided to call themselves The Billiard Balls.

Wednesday morning Mr. Diogen joined the club.

By Thursday more than half the boys were bald,

and the local paper sent someone to take their picture.

It would have been a great week, if not for two things: (1) the skull continued to insist something was coming to get it, and (2) for reasons Charlie couldn't understand, Mark Evans seemed to take each kid who shaved his head as a personal insult.

When Charlie mentioned this to Gilbert, his friend said, "Well, have you noticed that all the people who shaved their heads have something else in common?"

"What?"

"They want Mark's father to give up his plan to drain Tucker's Swamp. Maybe we should organize a protest march. Baldies to Save the Bog, or something."

"As if it would do any good," said Charlie glumly. He was beginning to understand that while not everyone in town approved of Mr. Evans's project, those who *did* approve were definitely in the majority.

However, Charlie was firmly convinced that was only because they didn't know the real truth.

On Friday Charlie went to school with nothing on his mind but the town meeting and the question of how to save the swamp. His attention was brought back to the here and now when he noticed someone else had joined The Billiard Balls.

Looking again, he was astonished to see it was Karen Ackerman.

"What do you think?" she asked, running her

hands over her shiny skull. She sounded proud, and a little nervous.

"I think you're amazing," said Charlie honestly, having learned a little something since the last time he was asked that question.

Karen seemed to take this as a compliment. "I was so scared when I did it," she whispered.

"I know what you mean," said Charlie.

"But I thought what you guys were doing was so...I don't know, so *right*, I guess...that I wanted to be part of it. Have you noticed how happy and comfortable Gilbert has been since you started this?"

"Not really," said Charlie. Then he added, very quickly, "But I'm not very good at that stuff."

"Good enough. So can I be an official member of The Billiard Balls?"

Charlie smiled. "I don't think we have official members. But as far as I'm concerned, you're in."

When Karen smiled back he almost said something embarrassing again, but managed not to.

That day at recess Karen hung out with Charlie and Gilbert.

"Hey, it's Swamp Boy and his band of baldies," said Mark Evans, when he went strolling past with a group of his friends.

"Me Swamp Boy. Me Proud Defender of Environment," replied Charlie solemnly, causing Karen to giggle.

"Defend all you want, Swamp Boy," said Mark. "After my dad's meeting tonight, your pet swamp will be as good as empty."

Charlie tried to come up with a suitable reply,

but couldn't. It didn't make any difference, because it was at that moment that he figured out how he was going to stop Mr. Evans.

"I'm not sure, but I may need to tell another person about you," Charlie said to the skull when he got home that afternoon.

"Cool! I could use a new audience."

"You think it will be all right?" asked Charlie, somewhat surprised by this response.

"Well, did the old man tell you not to? I don't know myself, since you never showed me his letters."

Charlie hesitated. "He just said to be careful what I said, and who I said it to."

"That leaves you a lot of room to maneuver. But remember, you'll still have to get whoever it is to look into my eye sockets and ask me a question before I can communicate with them."

"I know," said Charlie.

Then he went to call Gilbert.

"I'm sorry," said Mrs. Dawkins, when she answered the phone. "Gilbert's not feeling very well. He's sleeping right now." She paused, then added, "I've been meaning to thank you for what you did the other day, Charlie—about your hair, I mean. You're a good boy."

"Thanks," he whispered. He hung up, wondering just how sick Gilbert really was, and unsure whether he truly wanted to know the answer.

He sat in the hall for a while, then picked up the phone again. "Karen? Hi, it's me—Charlie. Can you

141

meet me behind the school in about half an hour? I need to talk to you. It's about saving the swamp."

Karen arrived on her bike. She was dressed in jeans and a dark blue T-shirt, and since she was totally bald, it was hard to tell whether she was a girl or a boy.

"What's in the box?" she asked as she sat down next to Charlie.

Hoping not to have to get into details, he said, "It's kind of a secret. But if you help me sneak it into the auditorium at the library, it may help us stop Mr. Evans from draining the swamp."

Karen looked at him suspiciously. "Is it, like, a stink bomb or something?"

Charlie shook his head. "It's not. I promise."

"Well then, what is it?"

Charlie hesitated. He could say, quite truthfully, that he didn't want to tell her. But he knew that would not satisfy her. "It's something . . . special," he said, somewhat vaguely. He paused, then added slowly, "If I show it to you, will you promise not to get scared or upset or anything?"

"What is it?" she asked again, more suspicious this time.

"It's nothing bad," said Charlie. "It's just kind of . . . *weird*."

"Hey!" said Yorick, in a voice only Charlie could hear.

"What *is* it?" asked Karen for a third time. She was clearly getting impatient.

Charlie took a deep breath. "It's the Skull of

Truth. He's sort of a friend of mine. The thing is, when people are near him, they have to tell the truth."

Karen rolled her eyes skyward. "Yeah, right. Look, if you don't want to tell me, just say so." She stood and started to walk away.

"Wait!" cried Charlie. "I'll show you!"

She turned back.

Charlie opened the box and took out Yorick.

Karen gasped. "Is that real?"

"Of course he's real!"

"But isn't that against the law or something? Where did you get it?" Her eyes widened. "Charlie, you didn't dig it up in the cemetery, did you?"

It was Charlie's turn to roll his eyes. "Of course I didn't. If you don't believe me, ask him."

"Ask who?"

"Him. The skull. His name is Yorick. Look him in the eye sockets and ask him a question."

"Charlie, if this is some kind of joke ..."

"It's not! *I promise.*"

She looked at him closely. "All right, I'll try. But if this *is* some stupid trick, let me tell you right now, I'll never talk to you again as long as you live. And that's a promise, too."

Charlie said nothing, just held out the skull.

Karen looked at it with revulsion. "Do I have to hold it?"

"I guess not. I just thought it would be easier. I'll hold it if you want."

She nodded. Then, looking into Yorick's eye sockets, she whispered, "Who are you?"

143

The sockets began to glow. Then, speaking in a voice that both of them could hear, Yorick said, "Actually, 'Who are you?' is a very profound question."

Karen screamed and scrambled backward. *"How did you do that?"*

"I didn't do anything," said Charlie.

"I didn't mean to upset you," added the skull. "It's just that I was thinking about it. I mean, you could say I am a child of the universe. Or you could say I am a profound mystery. You might even say—"

"Yorick, shut up," said Charlie.

"Sheesh. Some guys got no sense of wonder."

"Charlie," whispered Karen fearfully, pressing her fingertips to her hairless temples. "That voice . . . it was *inside* my head."

"That's how he communicates."

She looked at Charlie intensely. "How did you do that?" she asked again.

"I'm not doing anything. It's the skull. If you don't believe me, try telling a lie. You won't be able to."

"Okay, my name is—" She stopped, and her eyes grew even wider. "I can't do it!"

"Of course you can't," said the skull.

"Stop that!" snapped Karen.

Yorick sighed. "She's not being very gracious," he said, in a voice only Charlie could hear.

"Give her a break. She's not used to this kind of stuff."

"Who are you talking to?" asked Karen.

"The skull," said Charlie.

Karen turned to Yorick and said sharply, "If you're going to talk about me, I want to hear it."

"Make up your mind," Yorick replied.

Karen jumped, but then nodded. "Okay, I believe you. You're real. Where did it come from, Charlie?"

"Another profound question," said the skull.

"It's a long story," said Charlie. "I promise to tell you the whole thing later. Right now I just need to know if you'll help me sneak him into the meeting room at the library. I want to be sure Mr. Evans tells 'the truth and nothing but' when he talks about that swamp draining project tonight."

Karen smiled. "Why, what a lovely idea, Charlie!"

"I thought you'd think so. Now help me figure out how we're going to get this thing in there."

"I am *not* a thing," said Yorick primly. "I am a child of the universe."

"Is he always like this?" asked Karen.

"No," said Charlie. "Sometimes he's even worse."

"It's a gift," said Yorick smugly.

"Perfect!" cried Karen. "That's how we'll get you in!"

THIRTEEN

Down the Draining

Charlie shook his head. "What are you talking about?"

Karen smiled. "We'll disguise Yorick as a gift."

"Huh?"

"Look, you can't just walk into the library with a skull. And if you try to put that cardboard box up on the stage, someone's bound to open it to see what's inside. Either that or just throw it away."

"Heaven forfend!" cried Yorick.

"But if you put something that looks like a gift up there, everyone will assume it's for some sort of presentation and leave it alone. We may even be able to hide it right in the podium."

"Isn't that sort of like lying?" asked Charlie nervously. "I mean, it's not like we're actually going to give Mr. Evans the skull."

"You'd better not!" said Yorick.

Karen looked exasperated. "Of course we're not going to give him the skull! But we are going to give him a good dose of the truth. It's not lying, it's just...oh, you know—that thing magicians do."

"Misdirection?" offered Yorick.

"Is that the gimmick where they get you to look at one thing while the important thing is going on somewhere else?" asked Karen.

"Uh-huh."

"Then that's it."

Charlie looked at Karen nervously. "Boy, you're trickier than I thought."

"Do you want my help or not?" she asked impatiently.

Charlie smiled. "Let's go find some wrapping paper."

An hour later they entered the library, carrying Yorick in a gift-wrapped box. Charlie was still a little surprised, since he had half expected the wrapping paper to fall off, or the tape to refuse to stick, or something.

When they went downstairs to the theater the janitor was onstage, setting up an easel. He started to ask what they wanted, but Karen lifted the package, then put a finger to her lips. He winked at them and returned to his work.

Charlie looked at Karen in amazement. The whole reason he had told her about the skull in the first place was that he thought he would need her to create a distraction so *he* could sneak it into the room. And here she just walked in with it. He couldn't figure it out. As far as he could tell, he would have told fifteen or twenty lies by the time he got this far—or at least he would have, back in the days before he got the skull. Now he had no idea what he would have done if she hadn't been with him.

As they left the room Charlie glanced back toward the stage. He had told Karen the story of how he got the skull while they worked. Now some of the words from Mr. Elives' first letter flashed into his mind: *Under no circumstances should you let the skull out of your possession!*

"I hope I'm doing the right thing," he muttered nervously.

Charlie returned to the library an hour later with his parents and his uncle. The ride over had been a little tense, since Charlie's father was in favor of Mr. Evans's project, while his mother and his uncle were opposed to it.

Mr. Evans was already sitting onstage, along with several important-looking men, including the mayor. They were all dressed in dark suits and had extremely shiny shoes. Beside the lectern stood the easel, which now held a stack of charts and illustrations. Two microphones had been set up at the front of the room for people to ask questions, and a television crew had stationed itself at the back of the room. Charlie realized with a start that Dave was one of the crew. Because he had not yet decided how he felt about Dave, Charlie pretended not to see him.

The room was packed and the hum of voices

filled the air. Here and there a sharper tone broke through the hum as someone spoke loudly in disagreement.

Charlie saw several bald heads scattered through the audience. Two or three belonged to old men; all the rest were Billiard Balls from his class. Mark Evans, his head still covered with thick black hair, sat in the first row.

Though the meeting was supposed to start at 7:30, it was 7:45 before the mayor went to the lectern. "I want to thank you all for coming tonight," he said. "Though the truth is, I would have preferred it if we had been able to get this project moving without all this annoying fuss."

He paused, looking a little startled, then fumbled with his note cards for a moment. "We face an important decision as a community, a decision that could affect our economic well-being for years, even decades, to come. Harley Evans has developed a plan I believe can do great things for us. He is going to give us a brief presentation on the project, then answer any questions you might have."

Charlie glanced at Karen, who was sitting two rows away. She gave him the thumbs-up sign.

Mr. Evans rose to speak.

"As you all know, we have a problem here in Tucker's Grove. A lot of problems, actually, but most of them stem from the closing of the paper mill two years ago, which threw so many people out of work. Well, I believe I have come up with a solution to our unemployment problem."

He took the first card off the easel. Behind it was a large photograph of Tucker's Swamp. "This land is mere—"

He paused, looking as if he had forgotten what he was going to say. After an uncomfortable silence, he started again. "This land is not being used at the present time, except of course by the wildlife living there. However, those of us involved in this project really don't give a damn about a few frogs and turtles."

"I'll say!" shouted someone in the audience.

Mr. Evans blinked and glanced down at his notes. "Excuse me. What I *meant* to say is that we feel jobs are considerably more important than frogs and turtles. Now, if you will just look at this chart—"

He took down the picture of the swamp. Behind it was a graph with multicolored bars and lines. He spent several minutes explaining it. To Charlie's astonishment, everything he said was very positive. The town would get more jobs. More jobs would mean more prosperity, fewer family problems, greater this, better that, and so on and so on, until even Charlie began to wonder if the project was such a bad idea after all.

Was it possible the skull wasn't working?

Maybe Mr. Evans is an evil force greater than Truth, Charlie thought gloomily. He was trying to push down the even more disturbing thought that the project might actually be a good idea when he suddenly realized the real problem: It wasn't that the good things weren't true, it was that Mr. Evans was completely avoiding the negative stuff. He began to relax a little, confident that once people started to ask questions the whole truth would come out and the project would sink like a stone in the muddy waters of Tucker's Swamp.

Mr. Evans continued his presentation, showing artists' conceptions of what his industrial park would look like. It was pretty, in a stale, tame kind of way.

"I like the swamp the way it looks now," Charlie whispered to Uncle Bennie.

Bennie nodded. "I agree. Wild and strange—like me!"

At the end of the presentation, Mr. Evans said he would take a few questions. "Just stand up at your seat," he said. "One of the pages will bring a microphone to you."

Several people stood.

Charlie could barely keep from rubbing his hands with anticipation. This, he figured, was where they would put an end to the project for good.

The first questioner was a middle-aged man whose voice had a slightly desperate edge to it. "Mr. Evans, how many jobs can we expect this project to bring to Tucker's Grove?"

"Between four and five hundred."

A happy buzz filled the air. People applauded. Charlie scowled.

"How soon do you plan to start actually doing the work?" asked the second questioner.

"That depends in part on how this meeting goes," replied Mr. Evans, smiling broadly. That earned him a few chuckles.

151

Charlie began to squirm in his seat.

"Have any businesses actually said they would move here if you build this?" asked the third.

"We have commitments from four companies so far."

That was when Charlie realized what was going on. "It's *rigged!*" he said, louder than he intended.

His mother shushed him.

"It's rigged," he said again, softer but even more urgently. "Mom, no one is asking any tough questions. I bet the people with the mikes were ordered to only let people Mr. Evans had already picked ask questions."

"Oh, I doubt that's true," said his mother.

"Believe me," said Charlie. "What I'm saying is the truth. I can't—"

He broke off. To his horror, Mr. Evans had said, "I think we'll stop with that question." He glanced at his watch. "I have another engagement I have to get to, and—"

Charlie sprang to his feet. "I have a question!" he said loudly.

"This is only for adults, Charlie," said Mr. Evans smoothly. "I think you'd better sit down."

Charlie's cheeks were burning, and he felt like he was about to die of embarrassment. But he couldn't give up now. It was too important.

"Oh, go on, Harley," said a familiar voice. "Let the boy ask a question."

Charlie turned. It was Dave. He was holding a video camera, pointing it right at Charlie.

Mr. Evans scowled, then said, "All right, what's your question, Charlie?"

Charlie hesitated. This would be his only chance. He had to phrase his question the right way, so Mr. Evans couldn't wiggle out of it.

"What's your question?" asked Mr. Evans again, sounding impatient.

Someone began to laugh. Charlie felt his blush grow deeper. Every eye in the auditorium was drilling into him. He wanted to sink into the floor and disappear, or turn and run.

Trying to keep himself from fleeing, he remembered his father's frequent admonition: *Go for it, Charlie. After all, what's the worst thing that could happen?*

That was it!

"Mr. Evans, what's the worst thing that could happen if you drain the swamp?"

Mr. Evans smiled and spread his hands. "I suppose it depends on how you look at it. From a personal point of view, the downside is that I could be arrested for several violations of the federal wetlands law." Even as Mr. Evans spoke, his eyes were getting wide. He looked from side to side in desperation, but there was no one to help him. He kept talking. "From the town's point of view, there is a small but significant possibility that we could mess up the water table and ruin several hundred wells. Also, there are two species that could go extinct. But they're very minor, and of no real significance."

An angry buzz rose in the auditorium.

"Bingo!" cried Dave.

Charlie's mother looked at Charlie in astonishment as more questions were shouted from the audience.

Mr. Evans, blushing and stammering, began to answer, speaking slowly at first, then faster and faster. The truth that came tumbling out of his mouth was such a weird mix of good and bad that Charlie couldn't make any sense of it. Some of the answers generated applause, some cries of rage.

A fistfight broke out in the audience.

Suddenly Mr. Evans wrenched himself away from the lectern, cried out a truly sincere apology, and rushed from the stage.

To Charlie's astonishment, the startling revelations did not convince everyone that the project was a bad idea. As people were leaving he heard a man in front of him say, "Well, even if what Harley said was true, I think it's worth the risk. We need those jobs!"

"Oh, I don't think it was true, anyway," replied the woman he was talking to. "The poor man probably had a nervous breakdown because of all the negative pressure people have been putting on him about this project. It's a crying shame. I certainly hope this goes through anyway."

"Don't worry about it, sport," Uncle Bennie whispered to Charlie. "To quote an old lady we both know and love, 'Some people wouldn't know the truth if it walked up and bit them on the heinie.' "

Charlie smiled. His smile grew even broader when he spotted Karen making her way through the crowd. "We did it!" she whispered excitedly. *"We did it!"*

"Did what?" asked Charlie's mother. "What, exactly, have you two been up to?"

"We've been on a quest for the truth, Mrs. Eggleston," said Karen, her voice quiet and sincere.

Charlie's mother looked at them as if she had more questions to ask but couldn't quite figure out what they should be.

"Excuse me," said Charlie. "I have to get something."

Fighting against the crowd, he made his way to the front of the auditorium.

Mark was still in the first row, unmoved from where he had been during the presentation. His cheeks were wet with tears. "You come down here to gloat, Eggleston?" he asked when he saw Charlie.

"Not actually."

"Huh. I thought you'd be happy." He swiped at his face with his sleeve.

"I'm happy that the swamp probably won't be drained."

Mark's face twisted in disgust. "You're such a dweeb."

Charlie shrugged. "Probably." He glanced back at his parents, wondering what it would have been like to see his own father humiliated the way Mr. Evans had just been. "Look, I'm sorry that—"

"Shut up!" snapped Mark. "Just shut up!" He turned and bolted toward the stage. Charlie started after him, but before he had gone three steps Dave grabbed him from behind.

"Hey, hero—I need to get a little footage with you. Stand still so I can interview you!"

Charlie glanced behind him. Mark was already out of sight. He turned back to Dave, hoping he wouldn't be asked anything to which a truthful answer would be too embarrassing.

The moment Dave was finished with his questions, Charlie hurried onto the stage to retrieve Yorick. But when he stepped behind the lectern his eyes widened, and he felt a coldness clutch his heart.

The gift-wrapped box in which they had hidden the skull was gone.

FOURTEEN

Midnight Appointment

Seized by terror, Charlie hurried to the back of the stage. He began opening boxes, turning things over, searching desperately for any sign of the skull. With every spot that he checked, his panic grew deeper.

"Yorick!" he whispered urgently. "Yorick, where are you?"

No answer.

After a moment Karen joined him. "What's wrong?" she asked. "You look horrible."

"Yorick is gone!"

"What?"

"That box we put under the podium is missing. I have no idea what happened to him!"

"He must have been here during the presentation," said Karen. "Otherwise Mr. Evans wouldn't have said all that stuff."

"So someone took him afterward," said Charlie, trying to calm himself enough to think. "But who?

And *why?*" Suddenly he remembered Mark bolting onto the stage. "Oh, jeez!"

"What?" asked Karen.

"I think Mark took him."

Karen's eyes widened. "Why would he do that?"

"I don't know. Maybe he realized I had something to do with the box, and took it just to bug me. No, I bet it was simpler. I bet he figured it was something for his dad—maybe a gift the community was going to give him for coming up with his great industrial park. Oh, man. How am I going to get Yorick away from him? I'm dead meat, Karen. Mr. Elives gave me strict orders not to let anything happen to that skull!"

"Do you want me to call Mark?" asked Karen. "Maybe I can talk him into giving Yorick back."

"That *might* work," said Charlie, suddenly hopeful.

Karen put her hand on his arm. "I'll try as soon as I get home. Then I'll call you."

"Thanks," said Charlie, desperately hoping it really was Mark who had taken the skull, and not whatever great force Mr. Elives and Ms. Priest had warned him was after it.

The ride home was not easy. Though no one (except Charlie, of course) could figure out why Mr. Evans had blurted out so much truth, they all had something to say about it.

Mr. Eggleston, who had been in favor of the swamp project, was particularly upset by the revelations. He was also upset by Charlie's part in them. "Why didn't you just keep your mouth shut?" he kept asking.

When Charlie's mom pointed out that if Charlie hadn't asked his question, the lies would have continued, Mr. Eggleston grumbled and focused his attention on the road.

Uncle Bennie's clear delight about Mr. Evans's meltdown only made Mr. Eggleston crankier. Bennie himself seemed puzzled that Charlie didn't act happier.

But it was hard to be happy when he was nearly out of his skin with worry. His sense of triumph about getting Mr. Evans to speak the truth had turned to cold dread. He hoped desperately that he would find a message from Karen on the answering machine when he got home, telling him she had worked everything out.

Karen had not called. However, someone else *had* sent a message, as Charlie discovered when he entered his room and found Roxanne and Jerome napping in the center of the bed.

"What are you two doing here?" he demanded, terrified they would ask where Yorick was.

"What do you think we're doing?" replied Jerome sharply. He stretched and yawned, displaying more teeth than Charlie really wanted to see. "We've got a message for you."

"An important one," added Roxanne, preening her whiskers. "Otherwise we wouldn't have waited."

"What is it?"

Jerome glanced from side to side. Then he sat up, stretched toward Charlie, and whispered, "The old man says it's time for this to end."

"He sent you to get Yorick?" yelped Charlie, nearly squeaking in his terror.

"Yeah, right. Do we look like we could carry him back?"

"Be nice, Jerome!" said Roxanne sharply. Turning to Charlie, she said, in a more gentle voice, "Mr. Elives wants you to take Yorick to the cemetery tonight."

"Now?"

"Not now." She looked around, then whispered, *"Midnight!"*

Charlie glanced out the window. "The cemetery," he muttered. "Midnight. It figures."

"Don't blame us, kid," said Jerome. "We don't write 'em, we just deliver 'em."

"All right, tell Mr. Elives I'll meet him there."

Roxanne looked uneasy. "We didn't say *he'd* be there, Charlie."

"What do you mean? Why am I going, then?"

Before the rats could answer, the phone rang.

"Charlie!" called his mother. "It's for you!"

"I've got to take that," said Charlie, feeling a surge of hope. "It might be Karen!"

"Oh," said Roxanne knowingly, "a girlfriend. Come on, Jerome. Let's give the boy some privacy."

"Yeah, sure," said Jerome. "See you around, Charlie."

"Wait! Don't go yet! I need to know more about tonight, about the cemetery."

"We told you all we were supposed to," said Roxanne.

"Just make sure you're there," added Jerome sharply. He climbed down the side of the bed and disappeared underneath.

"Good luck," called Roxanne as she hurried after him.

Nearly sick with hope and fear, Charlie raced to the phone, praying it would be Karen with good news.

It was Mark.

Sounding triumphant, but also a little scared, he said, "Hey, Swamp Boy—Karen says I've got something that belongs to you. What are you dragging a skull around for anyway? And where did you get it from? Your father's butcher shop?"

"I need it back," said Charlie, ignoring the insult and fighting to keep his desperation out of his voice.

"So I hear. What will you give me for it?"

Charlie blinked. He hadn't thought in terms of a trade. "What do you want?" he asked.

To his surprise, Mark replied, "Actually, I just want to get rid of the darn thing!" Before Charlie could make a response, Mark let out a startled curse. "This thing is creepy, Eggleston! To tell you the truth, I wasn't going to give it back at all. But it scares me." He swore again. "I can't believe I just said that! Where *did* you get this thing?"

"It's a long story," said Charlie. Then, in a moment of inspiration he added, "But if you'll bring it to our old meeting place in the cemetery, I'll tell you all about it."

"After school tomorrow?"

"No. Tonight."

"What's the hurry?"

Charlie hesitated. If he told the truth—that he had to have the skull by midnight to save his own skin—odds were good Mark would keep it until tomorrow just to spite him. Especially since he had almost certainly figured out that the skull was responsible for his father's downfall, and that Charlie was responsible for the skull being at the meeting to begin with.

But the truth was the only thing he could tell.

Or was it? He suddenly wondered if it was possible that—with the skull not only out of his presence but also out of his possession—the truth curse might be broken.

He decided to try a tiny fib.

"Excuse me a second. I have to sneeze."

His eyes widened in delight. He had told a lie!

Turning away from the phone, he faked a monster sneeze. As he turned back to the receiver he thought, *Please let this work. Please, please, please. If it does, I'll never tell another lie as long as I live, skull or no.* Then, remembering what he had learned over the last few days, he amended the prayer. *Well, hardly ever. But I'll be a lot more careful about the truth. I promise!*

Trying to keep his voice from trembling, he put

163

on his most sincere tones. "The skull carries a terrible curse. Tonight is the only chance we have to return it to where it came from. If we don't, it will be with us forever." To his surprise, he realized that all that was the truth. But now it was time for the zinger. "Actually, it will have to stay with *you,* Mark, since you're the one who has it now."

"Are you serious?" squeaked Mark.

"I cannot tell a lie," lied Charlie.

After a long silence Mark said, "All right. I'll bring it back. When?"

"Meet me at quarter to midnight," said Charlie. Then, worried, he asked, "Can you get out?"

"No problem. I do it all the time."

Knowing that that had to be the truth, and not really surprised, Charlie started to relax.

He had barely put down the phone when it rang again.

"Well?" asked Karen. "How did it go?"

"I think it's going to be okay," said Charlie.

"Tell me about it," said Karen. "I want the details."

He repeated the conversation he'd had with Mark, and was absurdly pleased when he finished to hear Karen say, "Good work!"

Charlie sat in his room, waiting for the household to settle down. Sleep was out of the question. Fear seemed to flood his being. Even if Mark did bring Yorick back, what was going to happen after that?

At 11:40 he slipped out of his room and crept

quietly down the back stairs. Stewbone, who two years before would never have let anyone through the kitchen, lay sleeping as if dead in his corner. Charlie opened the door as silently as possible, then stepped into the backyard.

A light fog had begun to rise. It swirled around Charlie's feet. Despite the fog he could glimpse the cemetery stones through the hedge.

Charlie wondered if Mark would really be there, or if this was just a setup. He smiled at his own foolishness. "Of course Mark will be there. He's got Yorick now, so he had to be telling the truth."

He went to the designated spot, a tall monument anchoring a family plot that he, Mark, and Gilbert had used as home base when they played hide-and-seek here back in second grade.

Time wore on. Charlie paced back and forth. He checked his watch every few seconds, wishing Mark would hurry up. The night was cold and his sneakers were soaked with dew. He might have been tempted to just leave, if not for two things: (1) he was terrified of what Mr. Elives might do if he failed to return the skull, and (2) he had actually grown quite fond of Yorick—something he didn't want to admit but couldn't really deny.

After what seemed like hours (but was, in truth, only about five minutes) Mark arrived. He was carrying the box.

"Waiting for me, Eggleston?"

Charlie fought back a half dozen sarcastic remarks. Finally he just said, "Yes. Thanks for coming."

Mark snorted. "You're such a—" He broke off, looking startled.

Charlie smiled, realizing that whatever insult Mark had been about to fling at him must not be true. He wondered what it had been. Before he could say anything, he saw a flashlight beam approaching.

"Shhh!" he hissed to Mark, pointing toward the light.

"No need to be quiet for me," said a familiar voice.

"Karen!" yelped Charlie. "What are *you* doing here?"

"I wanted to see how this all came out," she said. "Besides, I thought you might need help."

"You were right," said Mark with a sneer. "He needs all the help he can get."

The fact that since Mark could say this it must be true did nothing to comfort Charlie. He was trying to think of a suitable response when they heard a whistle—three high notes, and one long, low one.

Charlie and Mark looked at each other in surprise.

"Gilbert?" asked Mark.

"You rang?" asked Gilbert, walking toward them out of the mist.

"You shouldn't be out tonight!" cried Charlie.

Gilbert scowled at him. "Karen told me you and Mark were meeting here. I figured maybe there should be a witness."

"What did you think I was going to do?" asked Mark angrily. "Kill him?"

"No. But I figured you might whack him around a little."

"Could you blame me, after what he did to my father?"

"He couldn't have done anything if your father had been telling the truth to begin with," said Karen gently.

Mark lifted the box, and for one terrible moment Charlie thought he was going to throw it. Darting forward, he cried, "Mark, wait! I wish..." He paused. "I wish..."

What did he wish? Whatever he said, it had to be the truth, now that he was back in Yorick's presence. Digging inside for the deepest truth he could find, he finally said, "I wish this had never gotten started."

"You wish *what* had never started?"

Charlie thought for a minute. What *had* he meant?

It must have been true, whatever it was.

"All of it," he said at last. "Your father's project. Me lying about it." He grimaced. "You beating me up." He paused again, then added sincerely, "Us being enemies."

Mark looked at him closely. "Do you mean that? The part about us being enemies?"

"I must," said Charlie, gesturing toward the box.

"Well, Swamp Boy, do you remember when we *started* being enemies?"

"Sure—back in second grade, when you got me in so much trouble with that toad thing."

"That's your version."

"What's yours?" asked Charlie, astonished by this comment.

"We started being enemies when I tried to apologize and you spit on me."

Charlie's eyes went wide. "Oh, my god," he whispered in horror. "I forgot about that."

"I didn't."

"Jeez, Charlie," said Gilbert, sounding disgusted. "I didn't know about that."

Charlie took a deep breath. "I'm really sorry," he said softly, and truthfully. "It was a creepy thing to do."

For a minute none of them said anything. Finally Charlie whispered, "I'm sorry about your father, too. I can't be sorry about the swamp. I love it. But I'm sorry your dad—"

"Shut up," said Mark. "You talk too much."

He stepped closer to Charlie, who braced himself, uncertain what Mark was intending to do next. But all he did was open the box. "Here's your skull," he said, lifting Yorick out. "Take the darn thing."

"Who are you calling a thing?" asked Yorick. Charlie could tell by the look in Mark's eyes that he could hear the words, too.

A smile twitched at the corner of Mark's mouth. "You know, I thought about keeping him, Charlie. But after half an hour of his babbling I decided if I really wanted revenge on you, the best thing I could do was give him back."

"Thanks a lot!" said Charlie, meaning two things at once.

As he took the skull from Mark, he felt a calm settle over him. It was only then that he realized how tightly he had been holding himself.

"Well done, gentlemen," said a voice from the mist.

Charlie yelped and spun round. Then he blinked in surprise. "Ms. Priest? What are *you* doing here?"

The librarian stepped out of the darkness and the mist. She was wearing a hooded cape. When she pulled back the hood, Charlie saw that she had a crown of daisies circling her head.

"I might ask the same of all of you," she said, looking in surprise at the group gathered there. "When Mr. Elives asked me to meet you here, Charlie, I expected to find only you and Yorick."

"Things got complicated," he said.

She nodded. "It is likely they did so for a reason."

"What do you mean?" asked Karen.

Ms. Priest reached out and took Yorick from Charlie's hands. "All four of you have been touched in some way by the skull and the truth it has unleashed on the world," she said. "So perhaps you were all meant to be here tonight."

"Why did Mr. Elives ask me to come to begin with?" asked Charlie.

"Follow me, and you'll find out," said Ms. Priest,

smiling mysteriously. She handed the skull to Charlie, then turned and walked back into the mist.

He looked at the others, shrugged, and started after her.

He could hear his friends following behind him.

The moonlit cemetery was quiet and still, the only movement that of the clouds overhead, which in turn made the shadows cast by the tombstones shift and change. As they walked on, the mist grew thicker, making it hard for Charlie to recognize where they were. Soon it was swirling around his knees, and then as high as his waist. Though he had played here since he was a small boy, he was totally lost. The stones surrounding them seemed taller—and older—than any he remembered.

Rounding a big willow tree (one Charlie could not recall having ever seen before) they came to the foot of an open grave.

At the far end stood a girl dressed all in white.

"You came!" she said, sounding pleased. Her voice, quiet and soft, seemed to scrape the marrow from Charlie's bones.

"We came," said Ms. Priest.

"There are more of you than I expected."

"There are more than *I* expected," replied Ms. Priest.

The girl looked directly at Charlie and said with utter certainly, "*You* are the Truth Bearer."

Charlie nodded.

The girl smiled. "Then will you follow me?"

Charlie glanced at Ms. Priest. Her face gave him no clue. He turned his gaze to Yorick.

"I'm game," said the skull, in a voice only he could hear.

Charlie lifted his eyes to the girl. "I'll follow," he said softly.

"Good." She turned to the others. "This is as far as you can come," she said, with just a hint of sorrow in her voice. "Charlie must go on alone from here."

"That's it?" asked Karen. "We just turn around and go back?"

The girl in white paused. She seemed to be thinking. Finally she said, "No, that's not all. You have earned the right to ask me a question."

"Why would we want to do that?" asked Mark. Then he added quickly, "And if that counts, don't answer!"

The girl laughed. "It doesn't count. And the reason you would want to do it is because I will give a true answer."

"You can't tell us what you don't know," said Gilbert.

"You would be surprised at what I know."

"All right," said Mark, stepping forward. "I'll start. What's going to happen to my father?"

The girl closed her eyes. "He will be sad. He will be happy. He will have great success. He will have painful failure. He will grow old. He will die."

Mark snorted. "That's not very useful."

The girl shrugged. "It's the absolute truth. If you want more specific answers, ask more specific questions."

172

Mark started to speak, but the girl shook her head. "You've had your question."

"But—"

Ms. Priest put a hand on Mark's shoulder. "You can have truth, or you can have mercy," she said gently. "Generally you cannot expect both."

Karen stepped forward. She glanced back at the others. Then, in a quiet voice, as if she was revealing a deep secret, she whispered, "Will I sell a book when I grow up?" Before the girl could answer, Karen added quickly, "I mean, one that I write?"

The girl smiled. "Yes, you will."

"When?" asked Karen eagerly. "How old will I be?"

The girl shook her head. "One question only."

Karen nodded, her bald head gleaming in the moonlight, and stepped back.

The white-clad girl turned to Gilbert. "Your turn."

Gilbert stepped forward, then stood in silence for a long time, looking not at the girl but down into the open grave. Finally he looked up and whispered, "Will I . . . Will I . . ." After a while he shook his head and stepped back. "Never mind," he said softly.

A silence hung heavy about them, broken only by the distant hoot of an owl.

"You are a wise child," said the girl. "And now the time has come. Truth Bearer, follow me."

Without waiting for an answer, she stepped into the grave.

FIFTEEN

Face to Face
(to Face)

Charlie gasped, expecting her to fall to the bottom. When she began a slow descent instead, he thought at first that she was floating. He stepped forward to look more closely and realized that the grave had a stairway inside—stairs that led deep into the earth.

He looked back toward Ms. Priest. "You must travel alone now, Charlie," she said softly. "I came to make the connection, but the journey itself is yours. I will escort your friends to their homes."

"Is it safe?" asked Karen, looking at Charlie with concern.

"Probably not," said Ms. Priest. "That doesn't really matter now. Charlie must do what Charlie must do, and we must let him do it."

Charlie turned to face her, to face his friends. "It will be all right," he said, and because he was holding Yorick he was pretty sure that was the truth, though what *all right* really meant he couldn't have said. "I'll tell you all about it when I get back." He paused, then added, "I'm glad you were here. *All* of you," he stressed, looking directly at Mark. He turned back to the grave. "Wish me luck."

"Luck," whispered Karen.

"Luck," echoed Mark.

"Luck, friend," said Gilbert softly.

Ms. Priest leaned close to his ear and murmured, "I shall wish you courage." Then she turned and led the others a distance from the grave.

Charlie looked at the girl, who was waiting for him three steps down. "Where are we going?"

"To my home."

Clutching Yorick tightly, he crouched at the edge of the grave, still afraid to enter. He watched as the girl went several steps deeper into the earth. She paused and turned to face him once more. As she did, a stray bit of moonlight illuminated her face.

To Charlie's astonishment she was no longer a girl, but a wizened old woman of extraordinary ugliness.

"Who are you?" he whispered, his voice thick with awe.

She smiled. "I am Truth."

Charlie gasped. The girl's gentle voice had changed to a harsh croak. He felt, for a moment, as if it might flay the skin from his body. Yet even as she spoke, she changed again, shifting into the form of a middle-aged man.

"I've been trying to come back to the world you know for a week now," he said in a deep voice. "Ever since you took the skull out of the shop. It wasn't easy, for the world has grown quite hostile to me during the last few years."

Truth turned and continued into the earth.

Charlie thought about turning himself—turning and running. He knew all too well how dangerous Truth could be.

Several things kept him from fleeing. Curiosity was one part of the mix. A degree of trust in Ms. Priest was another. But more than anything it was the feeling that if he didn't see this through, didn't enter the mystery opening before him, he would regret it for the rest of his life.

He put one foot into the grave and started down.

When he had descended several steps he laid his free hand against the earthen wall beside him. It was moist and cool. And solid. Sliding his hand along the wall, he traveled deeper, feeling sandy patches; cool, damp stones; fine, hairlike roots; the blunt ends of thicker roots that had been chopped off; and, once, a wriggling sliminess that made him gasp.

He traveled out of the moonlight, which had been streaming in over his shoulder, then stopped at the edge of a darkness more intense than any he had seen before.

Again he thought about turning back.

"Keep going," Yorick whispered urgently. "We have to keep going."

Reluctantly Charlie stepped into the darkness. No sooner had he done so than he saw a light ahead of him and realized that Truth was carrying a torch.

He wondered where it had come from.

The tunnel stretched on, slanting into the earth like a long throat open to swallow them. He glanced up. The flickering torchlight showed a stony roof, slick with moisture. From far away he could hear the sound of running water.

He shivered, feeling that he was descending into someplace deep and sacred. Then, suddenly, he felt nothing at all—at least, not beneath his fingertips. He extended his hand farther. The wall was gone. At the same time the glow ahead of him began to spread, as if the torch's light was stretching in all directions. They entered a place where all was mist, a mist so thick Charlie could see no more than a few feet ahead, despite the glow of the torch. Looking carefully, he could just barely make out Truth, who seemed to have taken on the form of a great lumbering beast.

Despite his limited vision, Charlie had a sense that the space they were in was vast and trackless. Were they still beneath the cemetery? Or had they gone someplace else, someplace stranger?

He hurried a few steps closer to Truth. At the same time he realized that the skull had been uncustomarily quiet.

"Yorick," he whispered. "Are you all right?"

"Fine. Just slightly terrified."

"I know the feeling," muttered Charlie.

Trying not to think about it, he focused on following Truth.

"Are we almost there?" whispered the skull, after another minute or so.

Charlie assumed Yorick was speaking only to him,

so he was startled when Truth answered. "Time is but an illusion. We will get there when we get there."

"Great," thought Charlie, directing his words to Yorick and hoping that Truth couldn't read his mind. "She—he—*whatever!*—is as annoying as you are!"

They traveled for what seemed like hours, though based on Truth's last comment, Charlie realized it could have been no time at all.

Suddenly he felt something jolt through him, a feeling of ice and electricity and hope and release.

"Uh-oh, Toto," said Yorick. "I don't think we're in Kansas anymore."

"We weren't in Kansas to begin with," replied Charlie.

"Sheesh. If you think Truth is annoying, you ought to try living with you."

The mist began to thin.

"Home," whispered Truth.

Charlie gazed around him. To his left was a wall of shifting, swirling mist. To his right reared a wall made of crystal, its surface alternating between areas so smooth and clear they were like mirrors, and other places studded with outgrowths so sharp that simply looking at them made you want to bleed.

Behind him was a wall of solid stone—which baffled him, since they must have just walked through it. The floor was made of stone, too, though in places he saw pools of water, or lapping flames, or holes that seemed to open into a great abyss. If the place had a ceiling, Charlie couldn't see it; the opening above them seemed to go on forever.

Truth walked to a spot halfway between the mist and the crystal, a square marked out by four large urns. Tongues of fire licked from one of them. Dirt was piled high in another. Charlie couldn't tell what was in the other two.

Positioning itself in the center of the square, Truth seemed to dissolve. But only for a moment. Suddenly it was a girl again, the one who had met them at the graveside.

"Thank you for coming with me," she said softly.

"Why have you brought us here?" asked Charlie. The question was not angry or fearful. It was just a question.

Truth, now a handsome young man, smiled. "I wanted to invite you to live with me."

"Me?" squeaked Charlie.

Truth laughed, a sound beyond description.

"Not you. Your friend."

Charlie wondered where the voice was coming from, for Truth had become a large stone. Then he realized that Truth had called Yorick his friend, which surprised him until he thought about it.

"Why do you want me here?" asked Yorick.

"I'm lonely," said Truth. "And I know two things about you. The first, Yorick, is that you sought me in your youth. The second is that you almost found me—came as close as anyone ever has. But you flinched at the last moment, and thus did not pass

179

the test. I had hoped you would. I had been rooting for you."

"Flinched?" asked Yorick.

"When the old woman you worked for in the forest asked if you thought she was ugly, you could not bring yourself to tell her the truth. And so she could not bring you to me."

"But that wasn't bad," said Charlie. "Yorick was just trying to be kind."

"Kind and unkind are no concerns of mine!" thundered Truth. "Nor am I concerned with good or bad. Many good things are not true. Many bad things are. I cannot change that."

With a hiss Truth transformed into a column of mist, stretching upward farther than Charlie could see. In a voice that sounded like swirling wind, and that seemed to hold the same sob that sometimes underlies the wind, it began to chant:

I am old as air, new as a baby's breath.

I am a prison. I am the key.

I am the knife that cuts, the salve that heals.

I am a weapon.

I am a gesture of peace.

I am longed for and hated, cursed and loved, sought and despised. More lies are told in my name than there are birds in the air.

I bring pain and I bring relief.

I bring sorrow and I bring joy.

I am what I am.

The column of mist began to spin. As it whirled, faces appeared in it, constantly changing, shifting.

"Stop!" cried Charlie.

Truth stopped.

Charlie looked at it in surprise. No one spoke for several minutes. Finally Charlie said, "I thought you'd be more... solid."

The column of mist laughed. "Pass your hand through me," it said in invitation.

Charlie hesitated.

"Go for it, kid," whispered Yorick.

Charlie stepped forward. The column was nearly two feet thick. He reached out, pulled his hand back. Biting his lip, he tried again. Extending his hand, he thrust it into the mist and began to move it sideways.

He got about halfway through when he ran smack into a core so solid it made stone seem soft. A shot of fear surged along his arm, seemed to shake his body. His mind reeled with scenes of horror and beauty. Sighs and shouts, screams and murmurs echoed in his ears. Darkness filled him. Light filled him. He staggered backward, fearing he might explode.

"I'm lonely," said Truth once again.

"I can see why," gasped Charlie.

"That's why I fought my way through tonight. I came to ask Yorick to be my court jester. I could use a good laugh now and then."

"Yoicks!" cried Yorick. "When I asked Charlie to take me out of the shop, I never thought *this* would happen."

"Of course you didn't," said Truth, in a thousand voices. "What you expected is not the issue. I make you an offer—a home with me, where you can speak what's true with no fear of harm or anger."

When Yorick replied his voice was unusually solemn. "I sought you as a youth, not to live with you, but so I could bring you to the world, which I thought was in need of you."

"As it is. But I can only touch the world in brief and fleeting ways. Were I to come sweeping across human lives, things would shatter around me. Look at Charlie: He touched my core for only an instant, yet he will never be the same. Had he flung his arms around me, pulled himself to me, embraced me, he would have lost all illusions forever. And how, then, could he have gone back to the world you know?"

A silence filled the chamber.

"Well?" asked Truth. "Will you stay?"

"I'm thinking," said Yorick. "I'm *thinking*!"

Truth burst out laughing.

"All right," said Yorick, sounding pleased. "I'll stay."

"Are you sure?" asked Charlie.

"I'm sure. After all, what is there outside for me? I mean, I like you, kid, but it's not like I'm ever going to have a big social life out there. And let's face it, you're not that fond of my jokes."

"And you think Truth will be?"

"I have a very strange sense of humor," said Truth. "Now, I think it is best for you, Charlie, to leave."

"How do I get home?" asked Charlie, thinking of the solid wall behind him.

"Take the side door. It will get you home more quickly."

Charlie glanced to his right. Though he had not

seen it before, there was a door outlined in the crystal wall.

"Where did that come from?" he asked nervously.

"The world is full of doors," said Truth. "Most people just don't see them."

"What about Yorick?"

"Toss him into my center."

Charlie stood, unmoving.

"Go ahead, Charlie," said Yorick. "I can take it."

"Are you sure?"

"As sure as I'll ever be. Besides, could I say it if it wasn't true?"

He lifted the skull so he could look directly into its eye sockets. They were glowing as brightly as he had ever seen them.

"Good-bye, Yorick," he said softly. "I'll miss you."

"And I'll miss you, Charlie. You know, I hadn't had a boy to pal around with since Hamlet was a pup. It was fun. Thanks for putting up with me."

Charlie started to say it was no problem, but couldn't.

He tried to say, "I enjoyed it," but found the words wouldn't pass his lips.

Finally he said, "I learned a lot from you, Yorick. I'll never forget it. Thanks."

He ran his hand over the skull's smooth dome one last time. Then, feeling a little silly, but also feeling that he had to, he bent his head and gave it a gentle kiss. "Good luck," he whispered. Stepping forward, he tossed Yorick into the swirling column of mist.

The skull disappeared for a moment. Then Charlie could see it again, whirling around, going higher, higher, ever higher up the column.

And in his head he heard, "Oh, my. Oh, *my*! *Oh*..."

The words ended, trailing into an extended cry, filled with delight and wonder, horror and astonishment.

Then silence.

Charlie stood and stared at Truth for a long time.

Suddenly the column of mist began to chuckle. The chuckle built, and built again, until Truth was roaring with laughter.

Charlie smiled and turned. Walking to the crystal wall, he opened the door and stepped through.

He found himself in the magic shop.

Mr. Elives was standing behind the counter, polishing it with a rag. When the owl on the cash register uttered a low hoot, the old man looked up and grunted. "Huh. About time you got here."

"He took the time he took," said Ms. Priest, stepping from the shadows. Standing behind Charlie, she put her hand on his shoulder.

"I notice you didn't bring back my skull," said Mr. Elives pointedly.

"I never meant to take it," said Charlie.

"I didn't say you did. But whether you meant to or not, you did. Are you intending to return it?"

Charlie took a deep breath. Ms. Priest squeezed

his shoulder. "I was going to," he said softly. "I truly was. But I met someone else who...needed it more."

"I believe the skull has been taken to its rightful home," said Ms. Priest.

Mr. Elives grunted. "That's all well and good, Hyacinth. However, the boy stills owes me something." He paused and looked at Charlie carefully. At last he said in a sly voice, "But you needn't worry about paying for it right this moment, Charlie Eggleston. I think I'd rather have you work it off."

"Work it off?" asked Charlie nervously.

The old man shrugged. "I need an occasional errand done out in the larger world. I would be willing to accept your help as payment for the skull."

Charlie glanced back at Ms. Priest, but found no answer in her face.

"Well?" asked Mr. Elives.

Charlie took a deep breath. "All right. That seems fair."

The old man nodded. "Good. You can go now, if you like. Take the side door. It will get you home more quickly."

Charlie was startled to hear the same words that Truth had used when he was ready to leave *its* home. He stared at the old man. Was that a smile on his face? It was hard to tell.

Turning, he looked at Ms. Priest.

She nodded.

Alone, he went through the side door—and found himself standing back in the cemetery.

Above him the sky was filled with stars.

The spring peepers were singing all around him.

His heart felt strange. He missed Yorick already. Yet at the same time, he was relieved to be free of him.

"Alas, poor Charlie," he whispered.

He rubbed his hands once over his bald and shiny head, then turned and started for home.

Epilogue

Charlie stood at the edge of Tucker's Swamp, listening with pleasure to the sounds of life pulsing around him.

"You almost ready?" asked Karen.

"In a minute," said Charlie. "I just want to let the fact that it's still here—that it's going to *stay* here—sink in. I still can't believe we saved it!"

"I can't believe it was ever in danger," said Gilbert. "People ought to be more careful."

"*You* ought to be more careful," said Charlie with a smile. "You're still pretty fragile, you know."

The fact that Gilbert had been fairly strong for the last couple of weeks made it all right to tease him this way. Charlie got a kick out of seeing the thin fuzz of hair that had sprouted on his friend's head. Unfortunately, he also knew that there were still no guarantees for Gilbert.

His thoughts were interrupted by the honk of a car horn. "Do you guys want to see this movie or not?" called Uncle Bennie.

Karen and Charlie helped Gilbert up the hill to where Bennie was waiting.

"That was a good movie," said Charlie a few hours later. "Only it was really sad."

"Hey, it's not called *The* Tragedy *of Hamlet* for nothing," said Uncle Bennie, who was sitting next to him on the couch. "You expected maybe a happy ending?"

"We thought it would have more about the skull," said Karen.

Bennie laughed. "The skull isn't even a character! It's just a prop."

"Alas, poor Yorick," sighed Charlie.

A honk outside indicated that Mrs. Dawkins had arrived to pick up Gilbert and Karen.

"Thanks for bringing the tape over," said Charlie, after his friends had left. "We'd been wanting to see what the whole story was about."

"Any special reason?" asked Bennie.

Charlie shrugged. "A friend told me it was pretty interesting. He was right. But then, he never did lie to me."

"You seem to be doing better in that regard yourself," said Bennie as he knelt in front of the VCR, waiting for the tape to finish rewinding.

"Truth and I are on much better terms than we used to be," said Charlie casually. "It makes things easier."

"You can say that again," said Bennie. He glanced at his watch. "I better get moving. I promised to pick up Dave at the station. He'll be finishing the late news in a few minutes." He grinned. "Hope he doesn't ask if I liked tonight's show. I'll have to tell him I was watching Mel Gibson instead. He hates it when that happens."

After Bennie left, Charlie said good night to his parents and went upstairs to his room. To his surprise, he found Roxanne and Jerome sitting on the bed, waiting for him.

"What are you two doing here?" asked Charlie, a little nervously.

"We've got a message for you," said Jerome.

"It's from Yorick," added Roxanne. "He sent it to the old man, and the old man asked us to bring it to you. So here we are."

"Do I have to sign a receipt?"

"Nah," said Jerome. "It's not like it's official business or anything."

The rats watched as Charlie unrolled the message, which was written on thick, soft paper.

Dear Charlie,

I thought you might like to know a little about my life with Truth, so I asked it to take a letter. I'd write it myself, only my handwriting isn't so good, on account of my not having any hands.

Anyway, life here isn't exactly what you'd call a picnic. Truth is very demanding, and pretty particular. And since it's writing that down for me, you can see it must be so. Fortunately, it does have a sense of humor.

Despite my gripes, I am basically happy. For one thing, I'm not so lonely anymore. (I wasn't lonely when I was with you, of course, but we both knew that wasn't a permanent situation.) So this isn't all that bad, despite the fussiness and uncertainty I have to live with.

Now listen, I've got an important bit of news for you. Truth has decided to give you a little reward for taking care of me until it could come fetch me. Get this: It says it has arranged things so that you will be able to compel truth from people just like I do—with one big difference. Your "power" won't be on all the time. (Truth says if it was, it would be more a curse than a blessing. I happen to know that this is so.)

What a concept: Charlie Eggleston, Agent of Truth. Is it a good idea? Hey, don't ask me. I'm just a fool. What do I know?

Speaking of knowing things—do you know why the eggplant crossed the road?

Write if you get work.

Yer pal,
Yorick

Charlie started to put the letter on his desk. To his surprise, it dissolved in a crackle of energy that seemed to wrap itself around his hand. He could feel the energy race along his arm, tingling through him like some weird electric shock. He shivered once, and then it was over.

He thought about what the letter had said.

Turning to Roxanne and Jerome, he asked carefully, "Has Mr. Elives mentioned me lately?"

"Oh, he's got big plans for you," said Roxanne. Her eyes widened in surprise even as the words left her lips, and she clamped a paw over her mouth.

Charlie smiled. It worked! Then, realizing exactly what Roxanne had said, he asked suspiciously, "What kind of plans?"

"Special missions," said Jerome. "He said something about sending you to Washington, D.C., on occasion."

Charlie's smile grew broader. Charlie Eggleston, Defender of Truth and Special Agent of Elives' Magic Shop.

It didn't sound half bad.

In fact, it might turn out to be kind of interesting.

And that was the absolute truth.

A Note from the Author

This book would never have happened if I hadn't got caught with my hand in the cookie jar.

Well, my hand wasn't exactly *in* the jar when I got caught. I was crawling along the counter with one of my mother's dense chocolate cookies, good but dry (I now think of them as "saliva suckers"), which I had removed from the jar against orders. When I heard my mother coming, I panicked and popped the entire thing into my mouth.

Mom stepped into the kitchen, saw me on the counter, saw my bulging cheeks, and said, "Bruce, do you have a cookie in your mouth?"

In a fit of brilliance, I shook my head and replied, "Mmmph. Mmm mmm mmph!"

I was punished, not for snitching the cookie, nor even for stupidity (which would have been appropriate), but for lying. Or, perhaps more accurately, for *trying* to lie, since I was so spectacularly unsuccessful at it.

The thing is, I was basically well behaved (this

brings snorts of derision from people who know me, but I swear it's the truth), and when I did get in trouble it affected me very deeply. In my case, I became unable to lie. I also became obsessed with truth, falsehood, the gray area between them, and how you negotiate this territory in the most ethical possible way. It can take a while for a writer to discover the themes that he or she is most fascinated with, but I have no doubt that, for me, truth is one of them. The inverse of this book's Charlie Eggleston is Rod Allbright of *Aliens Ate My Homework*, who is compulsively truthful. (Actually, Rod is based on me—right down to the bit about *l'affaire de cookie* and its aftermath.)

Even when my characters are not as truth obsessed as Charlie or Rod, they often spend time arguing with themselves about how they can be truthful and still manage to do what they want or need to do without getting in trouble. But, of course, the whole culture has this problem. On one hand, we give high honor to truth. On the other hand, we know the social value of the little white lie, the not-quite-true words spoken to spare someone's feelings, or avoid an unnecessary argument.

It's all very confusing.

Which is one reason I keep writing about it.